The Alpha's Caged Pet 2
Lillith Mykals Kennedy

THE ALPHA'S CAGED PET BOOK 2

First edition. February 3, 2022.

ISBN: 979-8201820961

Written by Lillith Mykals Kennedy.

Chapter 1

Alanis POV

It has been six months since I married Sebastian. So much has happened. I was afraid losing his sister would hurt Sebastian, but he pretends it never happened. I think it is easier if he ignores the pain. He says he understands why she was angry with him and hold the pain within him.

Sebastian spends all of his time focusing on his wolves and me. I do love the extra attention he dotes on me, but sometimes I wish he was not so consumed by me. He has spent so much time trying to find out who I am and where I came from, I am grateful. . We both were shocked to find out that my parents were not really my parents.

My parents told me about a tribe of wolves that were special. Each wolf had a gift in the tribe. My father told me I was a part of this tribe. When I was younger, I did not understand that I was a part of the tribe, but my parents were not. It seems they were assigned the task of looking out for me and making sure I grew into my gifts.

Unfortunately for my parents, they did not have a chance to groom me into my gifts. Alpha Raymond made sure of that. I wonder how much he knew about me and if that is why he kept me locked away the way he did. Was he afraid of me? Or maybe he had no idea what was going. If he had known what I was capable of, I do not think he would have locked me away, but I could be wrong.

Alpha Raymond's wolves did seek me out and want me for some reason, and I do not think it is because they liked looking at me in a cage. It is definitely something else. I think they need me for something. The wolves that belonged to Raymond are warriors, and to have someone that could heal them so they could keep fighting, well, that would be interesting and useful for them.

"Are you alright? You seem far away and deep in thought?" Alpha Sebastian asks me as he sets down a glass of orange juice for me on the kitchen table.

I look up at him and smile as sweetly as I can. "Thank you. You do not have to wait on me; I am capable of getting my juice, sweetie," I say.

He touches my chin, leans down to kiss me. Every time our lips touch, it feels like the first time we kissed. There is nothing that feels as good as being with him. He makes everything worth living.

He sits down beside me. "You did not answer my question," Alpha Sebastian reminds me as he reaches for my hand.

"I know, I think I am okay, but I am not sure. I was thinking about my parents and what you told me about them. They were always good to me. My mother tried to protect me when Alpha Raymond came for us. She loves me as if I was her own. I cannot believe that I did not belong to her," I say—the words sting as I say them.

My mother loved me and cared for me. I am not sure how long I was with her; we have not figured everything out about my childhood or my past, but we do know is that the tribe of wolves I come from are a dying breed, and I need to find out as much as I can as quickly as I can.

"Your parents loved you, even if they were not your real parents. Do not let anything we find out change how you feel about them. They raised you," Alpha Sebastian says. He holds my hands so tenderly.

"I know you are right, Sebastian. I love them, and I always will love them, but I need to know who I am. At first, I did not care where I came from, but now that I know I have an entire family, I know nothing about it; it is different. I feel like I need to know everything about them and myself. I feel like I do not even know who I am. What if we have children? What will I tell them if I do not know who I am?" I cry as I have a minor breakdown.

Alpha Sebastian maintains his always calm demeanor. "If you want to stop, we will. If you want to keep looking, then we will. As far as what you would tell our children, all they need to know is how wonderful you are, Alanis," Alpha Sebastian says.

His eyes are filled with so much love as he looks at me and smiles. He does genuinely love me. When I was trapped in the cage in Alpha Raymond's basement, I never thought that this would ever happen for me, but here I am, sitting with the man I love and discussing our life, my life, our possible future children, and it feels beautiful.

"I did not mean to have a complete mental breakdown this early in the morning. I am afraid and excited to find out who I am and where I came from," I say.

"Alanis, no matter what we find out, I will love you, and I will be here for you," Alpha Sebastian says.

"I know you will, and I love you so much for it," I say.

Alpha Sebastian laughs as he takes my hand. He pulls me over into his lap quickly. "Show me how much you love me," he says as he kisses my lips. His hand firmly holding me and pulling me closer to him with every intense moment of our kiss. My breathing becomes labored, and now all I can think about is him and being with him.

Just as I think this will be the perfect morning and I can spend it with my love, I hear someone come rushing through the front door, unannounced and in a hurry. Alpha Sebastian growls as I lay my head in the crook of his neck. Maybe he can get rid of them quickly, and I can be his this morning.

"My apologies, Alpha, but we found them," Jeremiah says as he realizes he is in trouble for interrupting us. Jeremiah is one of Alpha Sebastian's warriors. He is excellent at finding out things and locating people, wolves, or someone that does not want to be found.

I raise up quickly and look at Jeremiah. "My parents? Did you find my parents?" I ask him.

He shakes his head. "Do you want me to bring them here?" Jeremiah asks.

"Yes, will it be a problem?" Alpha Sebastian asks.

"No, the Alpha where they are located is not one of the tribe. He took the wolves in when they were left without an Alpha. It is much too much for me to explain. I spoke with him and his wife; she is like you, Luna. They are willing to have you both come to their home, or I can escort your parents here," Jeremiah says.

"What do you want to do?" Alpha Sebastian asks me.

"Are there others there like me?" I ask Jeremiah.

"Yes, there is a tribe of wolves like you. I am sorry, Alanis, but I cannot recall what they are called. I was excited for you when we found your parents and all of the wolves like you. It seems a lot is going on with them," Jeremiah answers quickly.

"We will leave this afternoon. Make the arrangements and get Dustin in here. I will need him to act on my behalf while I am gone. Jeremiah, I want you to go with us," Alpha Sebastian says.

"Yes, sir," Jeremiah says.

Jeremiah gets to the door. "Imperials, they are imperial wolves, and the Luna, her name is Kate," Jeremiah says; he smiles and goes out the door.

"Get packed, and I have a lot to do before we leave. Normally I leave Jeremiah in charge, but we need him with us. I believe Dustin will do fine," Alpha Sebastian says.

"I do too, Dustin is a smart wolf, and he always listens to you. He will do fine," I say. I kiss Sebastian and get out of his lap.

"Maybe if I hurry, we can continue this," Alpha Sebastian says as he pulls me back into his lap to kiss me deeply.

"I hope so," I say.

Chapter 2

Alanis POV

Jeremiah and Alpha Sebastian load the truck while I watch from the porch. I always enjoy watching Alpha Sebastian do anything. He always looks happy, smiling, and talking with people when he is not worried about his pack or me. Right now, he is only loading the truck; when we leave, he will worry about his pack and me.

Dustin brushes me as he goes down the steps. I can hear something coming from him, like on the inside. It is strange. I feel screams and then something cold, maybe sharp. The images are blurry as I feel the pain coming from him.

"Alanis, what is wrong?" Alpha Sebastian asks me. I suddenly realize I am lying on the ground, looking up at the clouds.

"I felt something coming from Dustin; it was strange," I say.

Alpha Sebastian, Dustin, and Jeremiah look at each other and then back to me. "What did you see?" Dustin asks me.

I close my eyes and envision what I see coming from him. It is hard to put into words when I am unsure what I am looking at, but I have to try to relay what I saw to Dustin.

"It looked painful, Dustin. It was blurry and painful. I am not sure how to tell you what I saw," I say.

Dustin reaches down and helps me up. I look into his eyes, and then I see it. I see Dustin dying in front of me. It feels real, and it seems real. I begin to scream loudly. Alpha Sebastian and Jeremiah grab me.

"Tell us, what is happening, Alanis," Alpha Sebastian demands.

"He is going to die," I say. I put my arms around Dustin. Dustin pulls away from me. He shakes his head.

"No, I have a wife and child. I cannot die," Dustin says.

"When? How?" Jeremiah questions me.

"I do not know. I see blood and a wound to his head. I feel pain in his arm, but I do not see anything else, just pain, and everything is so blurry," I say.

"Jeremiah, call Samuel. I want him to watch the pack while we are gone. We will take Dustin with us. If anything happens, Alanis can heal him," Alpha Sebastian says.

Dustin looks at me. "Are you sure I am going to die?" Dustin asks me.

I look at the ground. I close my eyes, and I see it all again. I hear screaming, and I think it is his wife screaming. "Yes, I am sure," I answer him as I lift my head.

"Come with us, Dustin. Alanis can keep an eye on you and help you if anything happens. We will make sure you live," Alpha Sebastian says.

"We should not change the future, Alpha," Dustin says. He goes back into the house to stay behind.

"He knows something is coming for him; should we wait? If someone is coming after the pack once we leave, then I can wait to find out about my parents," I say.

"No, Jeremiah, stay here. I will take Alanis. We will only be gone a few days. If anything happens, let me know. Let Dustin run the show. He needs to prove himself, but if any trouble shows up, take care of it," Alpha Sebastian says.

Alpha Sebastian and Jeremiah shake hands and then hug. It is strange, and they act as they will never see each other again. Jeremiah reaches for me then steps back.

"No offense, but if you are seeing people's death, I would like to keep mine a secret," Jeremiah says.

"I understand," I say. Jeremiah opens the door to the truck. As I get in, I make a point to touch his fingers on the door and then get into the truck quickly. I begin panting as I see what is coming for him.

I saw Alpha Sebastian out of the corner of my eye, watching me as I touched Jeremiah. He is curious too. He gets into the truck and drives out of the driveway quickly.

Alpha Sebastian stops at the stop sign about a mile down the road. "What did you see, Alanis?" he asks me.

I shake my head. "It is blurry. I have never had anything like this happen to me before, and it is scary. I need help from people like me. I do not know if I am seeing something that will happen tomorrow or ten years from now. Maybe the Imperials can help me," I say.

Alpha Sebastian shakes his head. He leans over and kisses my forehead. "It is not a long drive; we will get the information and get back home," Alpha Sebastian says. He reaches for me and then hesitates.

"I did not see anything when you kissed me. I think you are safe for now," I say. He puts the truck in drive, and we start our journey. I reach over and turn on the radio as Alpha Sebastian drives.

It is strange that I suddenly have some sort of gift to see someone in pain. I usually can heal, but this is unusual and makes me afraid. When I get to the wolf pack, I hope that their Luna and her people can help me.

"We know nothing about these wolves, do we, Alpha?" I ask Sebastian.

"Jeremiah and I did not have a lot of time to dig into them, but what I know is that the Luna is a lot like you, and she can help us. Maybe the Alpha can help me understand how I can help you," Alpha Sebastian says.

"What is her name?" I ask.

Alpha Sebastian thinks for a moment. "Kate, Luna Kate, and Alpha Erick. She has a lot of power, from what we gathered. She has a very powerful daughter, even more, powerful than Luna Kate. Alanis, this Luna can help you control what is happening inside you and teach you to use it correctly. It seems she had some issues when she came into power. I do not want that for you," Alpha Sebastian says.

"I will listen to her and accept her help, I promise you," I say to him. I unbuckle my seat belt and move over to him. I lay my head on his shoulder. I want to be close to him before dealing with all this wolf drama. I look up at him as he drives. He is concentrating on everything. I can see his worry. I am not sure if he is worried about his pack or me or maybe both.

Chapter 3

Alanis POV

I fall asleep beside my sweet Alpha. I am peaceful and content when we are together. For the first time in my life, I feel like I am in some sort of control. I am not in a cage, and I am with someone who loves me. Now, if I can figure out what is going on with me, then maybe Sebastian and I can move on with our lives.

"Alanis," Alpha Sebastian says softly. I open my eyes and look up to see a cabin. Several wolves are waiting for us as we pull into the driveway.

I do not want Alpha Sebastian to see my fear. I am not sure what it is I am feeling; maybe it is fear, but it is like a pull. I am pulled toward something or perhaps someone.

"I feel strange," I suddenly exclaim. Why did I say that? I shake my head as the feeling begins to take over my body.

Alpha Sebastian parks the truck and gets out quickly. He comes around to my side and pulls me to the side of the seat. "Alanis, are you alright?" Alpha Sebastian asks me.

I look up to see the most beautiful creature I have ever seen in my life. A beautiful woman with long dark hair and the greenest eyes I have ever seen in my life. "Who are you?" I say to her as she approaches me.

She smiles at me as Alpha Sebastian moves out of the way. I see her husband, the Alpha motioning for my Alpha to move. The two Alpha's leave us to get to know one another. "Kate," I whisper.

She touches my face. "Yes, I am Kate, and you, my sweet Alanis, are experiencing what it is like to come into your power," Kate says. I look at my hands and see so much energy and glowing matter. It is like I am looking at someone else's hand. Kate takes my hand, and we connect on a level that is unreal and like something I have never felt before.

"What is that?" I ask her. I am amazed at how calm she is and how in awe I am.

"That is nature, and it is using you. It will consume you and give you amazing powers that you will not believe. You have to harness every bit of it, or it will consume you in a bad way. I am going to help you be your best self, your best wolf," Kate says.

I watch the glow between us. "Thank you," I say. It is all I can think to say as I watch nature move as a force of energy between us.

"Come on, there is a lot to talk about, Alanis," Luna Kate says as she takes my hand and helps me out of the truck. I look behind me to see where Alpha Sebastian is, but I do not see him anymore.

"Erick took him to show him our land. It will keep both of them occupied for a while. It gives us time to get acquainted," Luna Kate says.

I smile at Luna Kate and follow her into her home. "My children are with the nanny so that we can talk about some things," Kate says as I follow her through her home. She opens a door just off of the kitchen.

"Your home is beautiful," I say to her.

"It was Alpha Erick's family home. I was a slave in this house at one time, and then I became Alpha, and now I am his Luna," Kate says.

"I was a prisoner at one point in my life," I say. I have shame when I talk about being in a cage. I do not know why it brings me so much disgust. It is the past, and I am not that person anymore, but I do not want to talk about it.

WE WILL NOT TALK ABOUT IT, a voice almost screams in my ear.

"I can hear your thoughts, and if you listen hard enough, then you will be able to hear mine and other wolves. You have an amazing gift. Honestly, I think you are more like my daughter than me," Luna Kate says.

"I am sorry, I hate talking about the cage," I say.

Luna Kate sits me down in a chair and takes the seat next to me. She is very calm. "Listen, Alanis, and you have to accept everything you have gone through and not push it down. It will consume you, and that natural energy that you have will turn black as night. You have to try to look for the good. Now we all have bad days, and we all have bad thoughts, but wolves like you and I have to be careful with our feelings and thoughts. The way we feel could hurt someone," Luna Kate says.

I shake my head. I try not to think about the cage, but she is right. I will never get over it if I do not deal with it. "I do not know how to deal with it. I went from the cage to be with Sebastian to dealing with another Alpha trying to take me, and I never dealt with any of it," I say. I lay my head over on Luna Kate and begin to cry. I hear the door open and look up to see a child. A beautiful little girl is looking in on me. She smiles at me and then touches me on the cheek.

"You will be good, Alanis. You are one of the elite wolves," the little girl says, and then she turns around and leaves.

I sit up, looking at the door. "Before you and Alpha Sebastian have children keep in mind that you could have a child that is as powerful as Belle, and it is a terrifying adventure. I would not trade being her mother for anything in this world, but I worry the world is not ready for wolves like her and like you," Luna Kate says.

I lean back in the seat. I know Luna Kate is listening to my thought. I try to think about everything I have been through from the cage to now. I have to deal with all of it, and it happens tonight.

"Kate, do you know who my parents are?" I ask her.

Kate looks at me, shocked, and she clears her throat. "Alanis, I can help you with your parents if you are sure," Luna Kate says.

I think about it and then look at her. "Yes, I want to know the truth," I say.

"I hope you can deal with yours better than I dealt with mine," Luna Kate says. What does that mean?

Chapter 4

Alanis POV

Luna Kate is extremely kind and answers all of my questions. I know I must be asking a thousand questions about who and what we are. What type of wolves and what kind of power do we have? I know all of this is like having a child asking her a million questions, but I need to know. I thought I knew who my parents were, but now I find out the wolves that raised me were not my parents. It is a lot to take in at once, but Luna Kate is trying to help me through it as we go through her pack records.

"You can trace your family here, see," Luna Kate says as she points to a wolf record from her pack.

"So your pack is here with your husband's pack?" I inquire.

"Yes, it is complicated, but we are all here on one territory. At least for now. It is not working out all that great. Our wolf pack is quite arrogant and selfish. You are not like that, I can see, but many of us are. I was at one time. I had a hard time. I almost lost my husband and my children, but I found my way, and you will too," Luna Kate says.

I look at the door to see Luna Kate's daughter, at the door again. She has peeped in on us several times. "She is intrigued with you because you are like her. She can heal wolves and so much more. She has a gift like yours, Alanis. You have to learn to use it correctly," Luna Kate says.

"What did she mean by I am an elite wolf, I do not understand?" I ask Luna Kate.

"It is difficult to explain, but I can show you tomorrow. There is so much to show you about the spiritual realm and how we have ancestors to help us. We are not just wolves; and we are witches and vampires. We have a unique bloodline, and you are part of the line my mother and father helped create," Luna Kate explains.

"Vampires, witches, and wolves, this is a lot to take in at once," I say.

Luna Kate sits down beside me, her beautiful daughter Belle joins her. They both take a hand and then join their hands. We form a circle, and the three of us are connected. "We are one," Belle says.

I can feel the energy from them passing through to me. It is strong. "Alanis, you are so strong," Luna Kate says.

The door to the small room we are in opens, and a tall wolf comes into the room. "Luna Kate, I need to speak with you," He says. He stares at me for a moment.

"Who are you?" he asks.

"This is Alanis; remember I told you about her. She is one of us, Conrad," Luna Kate says.

He rushes to me and takes my hand. "Hello Alanis, I am Conrad. I am an elite wolf just like you. I would love to help you in any way I can. Consider me at your service," Conrad says.

He takes my hand and kisses the top of it. I do not want to be rude, so I let him. I look up to see my sweet husband standing at the entranceway. He clears his throat. "Conrad, It is nice to meet you. This is my husband, Alpha Sebastian," I say. I do not want Sebastian to be upset in any way.

Conrad looks embarrassed as he turns to introduce himself to Alpha Sebastian. "I meant no disrespect. We are from the same wolf tribe. I only want to be of service to her and you, Alpha," Conrad says.

"Of course," Alpha Sebastian says. I can tell he is a little pissed, but he handles it well.

Conrad leaves quickly but takes one last look at me and smiles before he leaves the room. "Nice to meet you, Alanis; I hope we speak again," Conrad says. Alpha Sebastian growls but quickly stops. He does not want to disrespect Alpha Erick or Luna Kate in any way.

"He is harmless, I promise," Luna Kate says.

"She is right. He is one of the few elite wolves Luna Kate has anything to do with. The wolves are here, all of the imperials, but the elite wolves, the ones that follow the weeping wolf, they are very different than the imperials," Alpha Erick says.

I am confused, and I am sure I look confused. "I do not understand any of this," I say.

"I promise you will. I plan to give you a crash course tomorrow, and if you still want me to, I can help you with your parents," Luna Kate says.

I look at Sebastian, my sweet husband. I want him to reassure me, but he is watching Conrad leave. Indeed he is not that jealous. He knows he has my whole heart, and I would never cheat on him. "Alpha Sebastian, what do you think?" I ask him.

Sebastian returns his attention to Kate and me. "Are her parents still alive?" Alpha Sebastian asks.

Luna Kate hesitates and then takes a deep breath. I know that there is a reason she is reluctant, and maybe I should walk away from this part of finding myself, but I need to know. I want to know where I came from and who my parents were or are if they are alive. Is it too much to ask?

"We can talk about my parents tomorrow. Maybe it is best if I do not know who they are or where they are," I say.

I get up and walk toward my husband. I want to be in his arms. I fall into him. I want to cry, but this is not the place for a Luna to have a meltdown. I feel a soft touch and turn around.

"They are alive, and I will take you to them tomorrow, okay," Luna Kate says. This revelation gives me hope.

"Thank you," I say.

"How about we get something to eat," Alpha Erick suggests.

Alpha Sebastian and I follow Alpha Erick and Luna Kate to the dining room for dinner. This has been a long exhausting day. I need to eat and sleep. Tomorrow I get answers.

Chapter 5

Conrad POV

I have waited for her for so long, the mate that was taken from me, my Alanis. She was promised to me when we were children, but her parents, those fools, broke my heart by sending her away. I was only a child when I lost my mate. No child should be told that they will have to be alone because the mate they were promised s being sent away. They defied the weeping wolf and should be punished for coming between Alanis and me. They have to pay. I need to get to them before they have a chance to tell Alanis anything about my family or me. They have to be silenced. They will be silenced no matter what it cost me.

Alanis's parents had no right to interfere with fate. She was my fated mate. The weeping wolf chose us to be the elite Alpha family. We would produce elite wolves to rule over the imperials and they did not want that. The imperials are afraid of the elites, and now they will pay. I will kill them and take Alanis.

There is no way that Alpha loves her the way I would love her. I would worship the ground she walks on and keep her safe. He can never keep her safe from the imperials or from herself. She does not even know how to control her power. She could hurt herself.

We would have elite wolf cubs and rule the imperial pack. I love her, and I cannot take another day being away from her. After smelling her scent and seeing her after all these years, it has ignited a fire within me, and I have to have her. I long for her, not only her body but everything about her. She will be mine.

"Conrad," I hear a voice calling out to me. I look behind, but no one is there. "Listen to me, carefully, behave yourself. I am coming to help you, be patient and wait for me," the small voice says. It is another elite wolf warning me. I have to cover my thoughts. I have to seek out the weeping wolf for help. Only the weeping wolf can interfere and save Alanis from herself. She needs to be kept safe.

I walk back to my cabin. It is on the south side of the pack territories, right in between the wolves that love Luna Kate and Alpha Erick and the ones that hate Alpha Erick. Some wolves feel Alpha Erick does not care about the imperials, and maybe he does not. I could care less what he thinks about the elite wolves or me. All I care about is Alanis, my sweet Alanis.

"Watch yourself," I hear the voice whisper again. I go into my cabin and sit down in my chair. I want to scream! Just as I am about to lose my mind completely, there is a knock at my door, a soft knock, and before I can say come in, the door opens, and a small wolf is standing at my door. A small she-wolf, beautiful and all-white, is looking at me. She stands in the doorway for a moment and then quickly shifts into a woman.

She walks across the room to me, completely naked. She stops in front of my chair, looks at me, and then straddles me while looking into my eyes. She is beautiful. Her long white hair and pale haunting blue eyes make her look otherworldly and damn beautiful. She leans down and kisses me on the lips so softly.

"I am Iris, and I am here to help you, Conrad. I will help you retrieve your mate and take your place as the Alpha of the Elite Wolves and ruler of the Imperials. Do you want my help?" Iris asks me. She is hypnotizing. It takes me a moment to form a sentence. I cannot believe how beautiful she is and right in front of me. I have never seen any wolf that looks like her.

"Yes, I want your help, but what do you want in return for helping me?" I ask her. She giggles as she moves her body over mine. She leans down and kisses my ear.

"I want an elite baby. You give me a baby, and I will give you everything you have ever desired," Iris says.

"You want me to give you a baby, and that is all?" I ask her.

"Yes," She moans as she kisses down the side of my neck.

I grab her by the wrist. "I have saved myself for Alanis, and I am a virgin, Iris. I will not give myself to a wolf I do not know," I say to her.

Iris breaks free from me. She kisses me again and moves her body over mine, grinding me harder. "Either fuck me or stay a virgin because, without me, you will never get Alanis. This is business. I need your seed, and that is all, but I need it now. My body is primed and ready to conceive. Decide quickly, Conrad. I am sure I can find an elite to seduce tonight, but you, Conrad, you need my help and it would be fun to help you. Plus, you are special. We both know how truly special you are and how special your cubs will be so give me the seed or I can be on my way," Iris says.

"Okay, I will do it, but you have to help me get Alanis. I need your word that you will help me after I fuck you," I say.

"You have my word, Conrad. You will have Alanis in your bed very soon, but first, take me to your bed and put an elite cub in my womb," Iris says.

She wraps her body around me as I stand up, taking her to my bed. This is not what I want, but if I give her a cub, then she gives me Alanis.

Chapter 6

I hoped we would not have to be here very long, but it seems there is a lot for me to learn about the type of wolf I am. It all seems odd to me, but I must meet my parents. I need to know why I was raised by someone other than them. Why did they give me away? Are they like me? I have so many questions.

Luna Kate did look concerned about me meeting them. I should ask her why, but would it really make a difference. My Alpha, my sweet husband, is being so encouraging about all of this, and I trust him. If Sebastian thinks I should meet with my parents, then I will listen to him and meet with them. I know I turn to him a lot and put a lot on him when at times I should make my own decisions, but number one, he is my Alpha and my husband, and number two, I am afraid of making a mistake. I need his guidance.

"Are you ready, sweetie?" Alpha Sebastian asks me. He reaches out and takes my hand. This morning, we had breakfast in bed instead of meeting with Alpha Erick and Luna Kate. I needed to be with him for a little while before I meet my parents.

"I think so. I am excited and afraid, both. I want to know them, and I have so many questions, but I know the people that raised, they loved me, and they will always be my parents. Am I wrong for wanting to meet with them?" I ask Alpha Sebastian.

Alpha Sebastian pulls me close to his chest. I love when he holds me like this. He always looks out for me and takes care of me. "Listen to me, my love. I believe you need to know your parents. It does not make the people that raised you any less your parents, but there is something special about you, and we need to know how to deal with it properly. Ask Luna Kate what happened to her. She almost lost everything. The power you have is dangerous and you need to know everything about yourself. I will be with you and help you through all of this," Alpha Sebastian says. He leans down and kisses me gently on the forehead.

"I do not deserve you. You are too good to me," I say, laying my head on his chest. I want to curl up next to him and never let go, but I know that I have to deal with all of this first. I have Luna Kate to help me sort out my powers, and then my sweet Alpha and I can go home to work all of this out from there.

There is a knock at our bedroom door, and then it opens. I look over to see the little girl, Belle, standing in the doorway. "Luna Alanis, may I come into your room?" Belle asks softly. I nod yes. She looks like she is on a mission. Luna Kate quickly runs up behind her.

"I am sorry if she is intruding on the two of you," Luna Kate says. She takes Belle's hand. Belle pulls away.

"I have to tell her," Belle says, looking up at Kate.

"No, Belle, stay out of it," Luna Kate scolds her.

"It is okay, and she is not intruding. We are coming out now," I say to Luna Kate.

Luna Kate is annoyed with her daughter but handles her well. I cannot imagine raising a child like Belle. Damn, is that why they got rid of me? Maybe they did not want me to come into my powers, but why? Belle smiles at me. She is reading my mind.

"That is not what she is wanting to tell you, Luna Alanis, but what you are thinking is correct. Your parents sent you away to mask your energy and your powers," Luna Kate says. She looks upset by it.

"Are you angry with my parents?" I ask.

Luna Kate crosses her arms. "I was abandoned by my pack and raised by a man who gave me to the Alpha because he was indebted. I did not know how to turn into a wolf, and I knew nothing about my people. I learned the hard way and the hard way almost cost me everything. I do not want this to happen to anyone else. I want you to grow into your powers with help. So, I guess the answer is yes, your parents really piss me off," Luna Kate says.

I can feel her pain, and it stings all over my body. Belle looks uncomfortable, so it must sting her as well. "Tell her, mom," Belle insists.

Luna Kate looks down at Belle and gives her this look that only a mother could give. Belle slowly backs out of the bedroom. No matter how powerful Belle is, she still obeys her mother. I cannot blame her. Luna Kate scared the hell out of me.

"I will let Belle tell you what she is so anxious about when we return from seeing your parents. There is no need to let something happy be overshadowed by something terrible. Let us get the terrible out of the way first, and then we will deal with the happy," Luna Kate says.

I try to read her mind, but she has whatever it is blocked. "At least you are trying to use your powers, Luna Alanis, but I know how to hide my thoughts, and so does Baby Belle," Luna Kate says.

Alpha Sebastian and I follow Luna Kate out of the bedroom, holding hands. "I am excited," I say to him.

"Good, I want this to be a joyous moment and not hell for you. I hate when you are upset," Alpha Sebastian says.

"Luna Kate does not think it will be a happy moment," I say.

"No matter what happens, it will be good because you will have an answer to that question burning in your mind, and then we can move on to the next step," Alpha Sebastian says.

We go out of the house. Alpha Erick is waiting for the three of us. He is talking to Conrad and a woman, a very beautiful woman. She reminds me of someone, but I am not sure who. She turns and looks at me; she smiles. She steps away from the Alpha and walks over to me.

"Hello Alanis, I am Iris," she says softly. She extends her hand, and I take it. She looks at Alpha Sebastian. I'm not too fond of the way she is looking at him. "Hello," she says, almost growling as she reaches out to shake his hand. Conrad quickly joins her.

"Hello again, guys; I see you two met my future wife," Conrad says.

"Yes, we came to talk to the Alpha about getting married," Iris says, still eyeballing my husband. I look up to make sure Alpha Sebastian is not paying her any attention, and he almost seems to be under her spell. I take his hand, and he breaks from looking at her.

"Nice meeting you both," Alpha Sebastian says; he pulls me away.

"What the hell was up with you and her?" I ask him. He shakes his head.

"There is something about her, I know her, or something," Alpha Sebastian says to me.

"Let's go," Alpha Erick hollers to us. Luna Kate is already in the truck.

"We will have this conversation later," I say to him. I am furious, but not sure why. My emotions seem to be exploding. Alpha Sebastian leads me to the truck. It is time to meet my parents. I will deal with him later.

Chapter 7

Alanis POV

Alpha Sebastian holds my hand as we ride in the backseat of the truck. I look up at him occasionally. I want to ask him how he knew her, but it should not be something I am worried about right now. The only thing I should be worried about right now is meeting my parents. I have so many questions for them, but instead, I am riding in the truck scared and worried that my amazing husband is interested in another woman.

Luna Kate looks back at me; she touches my hand, then smiles at me. Her eyes beam with happiness for me. "Let it go. It is nothing. Relax your mind and just listen," Luna Kate says.

I give her a small smile and try to communicate with her in my mind. I relax and listen. I can hear her, but more importantly, I can listen to Alpha Sebastian. I can listen to his worry for me. I can hear his love in his mind, and it is all for me. I slide closer to him and let go of all my anxiety about Conrad and his soon-to-be wife.

We pull into a small cabin. There are several cabins lined up, and I can see a stream running behind the cottages. I notice one cabin is unused and looks rundown. "Before we go into the cabin, prepare yourself. I do not know how they will react. They are anti-elite wolves, and you are one of the wolves that terrify wolves like your parents. I understand. It is a scary situation, but wolves like you, like me, and like my daughter, we can all control our powers. Now, some elites have gone bad, very bad, but I know, Alanis, that you will be a great elite wolf, and I hope they see it too.

"I am ready for this," I say softly.

"You can leave any time, and no one will fault you if you get upset. Go with your heart, and honestly, do not expect much," Luna Kate says.

"Okay, I only want to ask them one thing," I say.

"I know, and they may not answer you about any of that," Luna Kate says. She glances at Alpha Sebastian and then smiles at me.

"Okay, enough of the pep talk, let's go," Alpha Erick says. I am not sure if he is being serious or kidding. He is hard to read. One thing about him I do know, he loves his family.

We get out of the truck and walk toward the cabin. An older woman begins walking toward us. I can see her out of the corner of my eye. I turn to look at her quickly. "Alanis, is that you?" the older woman asks.

I am not sure what to do. Luna Kate quickly steps in between us. "Maria, she is here to see her parents, and then you can speak with her," Luna Kate says.

Maria looks toward the cabin. "Jasmine and Walter have had a lot of company today. That is unusual. They never open their door for anyone, but today it has been non-stop people coming in and out," Maria says.

Luna Kate looks over toward Alpha Erick and Alpha Sebastian. "Maybe you two should check the house first, before Luna Alanis and I go inside. Just to be on the safe side," Luna Kate says.

Alpha Erick nods his head. Alpha Erick and Alpha Sebastian walk toward the house cautiously. Luna Kate reaches for my hand and takes it in hers. Maria stands with us as we wait. "Maria, did you recognize any of the wolves that came to the house today?" Luna Kate asks.

"Just one. That wolf, the other elite, what is his name? Let me think. Oh, yes, Conrad. The first time he was alone and the second time he had a she-wolf with him," Maria says.

"Are you sure?" Luna Kate asks Maria.

"Yes, I am positive. He used to come by a lot, but he has not been by in months, and then last night, he came by and twice today. You know they had a big falling out over their daughter and him being mates or something like that. I did not know they had a daughter except for you, Alanis. Of course, I am an old woman, and maybe I am confessed," Maria says.

Alpha Erick and Alpha Sebastian are both still inside the cabin. I am getting worried. "What do you mean by mate?" I ask.

"Conrad was confused about some things that happened a long time ago. He felt that he was mated to another elite, but it could not be. Mates are not decided that young, and you were moved at a very young age. You would not have been mates, but I thought he was over all of that. I spent a lot of time with him working through all of it so that he does not make his powers toxic. As I said, the wolf is harmless," Luna Kate says.

Alpha Sebastian and Alpha Erick come out of the cabin. My sweet Alpha looks almost as pissed off as Alpha Erick. Alpha Erick takes Luna Kate to the side to tell her what is happening. Alpha Sebastian stands in front of me, not saying a word.

"What happened?" I finally ask him.

"I want Luna Kate to tell you," Alpha Sebastian says.

I hear Luna Kate and Alpha Erick speaking, and I try to open my mind to listen, but Alpha Sebastian touches my hand and shakes his head. "Do not do that. Wait for a moment and let her tell you what is going on in there," Alpha Sebastian says.

Luna Kate comes over to me after a few moments. "Luna Alanis, I am sorry to inform you, but your father, Walter, is dead, and your mother, Jasmine, is missing. There is blood everywhere inside the house. Our pack will begin looking for her immediately, but the three of us think it would be better if you come back to the packhouse with me for your own safety," Luna Kate says so calmly it scares me. There is more to this, and no one wants me to know what it is.

"Okay," I say. Alpha Sebastian leans down and kisses my forehead.

"I am going to help Alpha Erick. You go with Luna Kate," Alpha Sebastian says.

"Okay," I say.

Luna Kate takes me by the arm, and we walk to the truck. We leave the two Alpha's at the cabin to look around. "I will send back some wolves to help them," Luna Kate says. I lay my head back into the seat and close my eyes. I am not sure if things are worse or better.

Chapter 8

Luna Kate POV

I watch Luna Alanis as we leave. I can feel her worry for her Alpha and for the mother she does not even know. She seems to feel so much, and that is terrifying. Her elite powers could grab ahold of that worry and produce something so volatile that no one would be able to help her. I have got to help her fine-tune her gifts and make the best out of this situation she finds herself in right now.

"Tell me about her," Alanis says in almost a whisper.

What do I tell her? "That is complicated, Alanis. The elite wolves and the Imperial wolves have a bizarre relationship. We all belong to the same pack, but the two are very different. Wolves, like you and my daughter, are strong and have so many abilities that it scares the hell out of everyone. Your mother was afraid of you and your abilities. She thought by sending you that far away that she could save you. The thought of sending a child away makes me angry. Alanis, I cannot be angry. I cannot give in to that rage that almost cost me my family. That is why it is hard for me to talk about your parents," I say to her. Her eyes widen.

"I understand. Maybe it is best that I do not know Jasmine and that my father is dead. I hate to say that or even feel that, but my parents. The ones that raised me, those are the ones that I love and will cherish. I guess maybe Jasmine and Walter are not important after all," Alanis says.

I am happy to hear her coming to terms with it, but there is one thing I am forgetting. Her parents were important enough for someone to kill one and take the other before she could meet them, and I want to know why.

"Can I ask you something, Luna Kate?" Alanis asks me.

"Sure," I answer.

"What happened when you lost yourself?" she asks. I do not want to go into all the details, but it is crucial to help Alanis, and maybe she can learn from my mistake.

"We have this voice inside us that guides us as imperials and elite wolves. The elite voice is much stronger than the imperial. It is a connection to nature, and it is magical. Remember, both of us came from a line of vampires, witches, and wolves. We are a hybrid like no other. My mother fine tuned that breeding to almost perfection, and that is why she was killed by the same people she thought loved her and wanted this perfect breeding. Those three things almost fight one another for control inside you. It is important the darkness does not win because if it does, you will face what I did. I lost myself and almost killed my husband. It is hard to talk about, but it is important," I say to her.

Alanis looks at me and then looks away. Her eyes begin to fill with tears. I can feel the pain inside of her. "You were angry with him and did not trust him. You begin to think he was cheating on you. Is that what happened?" Alanis asks.

I shake my head. "Yes, I felt like Alpha Erick wanted my best friend and that he was going to hurt me. None of it was true. I completely lost myself. He brought me back. He pulled me out and showed me his love. He did not give up on me, our family, or our love for one another," I say.

Alanis sits quietly for the rest of the ride to the packhouse. I can see the wheels spinning in her mind. Something happened. I cannot see it. She is blocking it well. At least, that is one thing I will not have to teach her how to do.

When we get to the packhouse, I park the truck. I sit in silence for a moment. Alanis finally reaches over to open the door of the truck. I reach over and touch her. "Wait, tell me what happened with you and Alpha Sebastian," I ask her.

She lets go of the door handle and takes a deep breath. "It was strange when we met Conrad and Iris. Iris spokes to him in a way, and he seemed off. Then he said he thought he knew her from somewhere. I was angry, and I wanted to kill him and her. The urge was strong, but the Alpha Erick hollered for us to come onto the truck, and I snapped out of it somewhat. I was still angry, but not as angry," Alanis says.

"Does he know Iris?" I ask her. Alanis shrugs her shoulders.

"I am not sure if he does or not. I do not know her. She does not look familiar to me at all," Alanis answers.

"She is a strange little wolf, she is an imperial, and she flirts with the elites. I figure she is trying to rope Conrad just to pop out an elite pup. It does not exactly work that way. She will not listen to anyone. She just floats around trying to seduce the elite wolves. She left this pack for a while and went to another, and then she came back when you came here," I say. I wonder if she had anything to do with Jasmine and Walter's disappearance. Why in the hell is she tangled up with Conrad?

"You think she killed my birth father?" Alanis asks. I almost forgot she has the ability to look into my mind. I know to be careful around Belle, imperials, and elites. I guess for a moment, I was not mindful. I will have to be more cautious around Alanis.

"I am not sure what I think, Alanis. I know that there are many things not making a lot of sense right now, and Iris is one of them. If she was flirting with your husband, she might be trying to push you over the edge. I want to know why she is doing it and what she stands to benefit from it if you snap," I say.

"My Sebastian is loyal to me," Alanis says. She smiles as she says it. Good, if she is confident in her love for him, then Iris cannot shake her up.

"Remember that the next time she is around, and make sure she knows that she does not bother you. Come on. We have got to find Jasmine," I say.

Alanis and I get out of the truck and go into the pack house. I send a couple of teams of wolves to help Alpha Sebastian and Alpha Erick. Hopefully, we can get this figured out soon.

Chapter 9

Alpha Sebastian POV

Alanis looks so broken as she leaves with Luna Kate. I am not sure if it is because she wanted to meet her parents or just the thought that someone took them and made a choice for her. Maybe we can find Jasmine and at least give her that. She was already on edge after meeting Iris with Conrad at the packhouse. She does not need anything more stress to add to her worry.

Alpha Erick waits until Luna Kate, and Alanis are gone. Then he pats me on the arm. "Come on, there is one thing about these wolves that is not like us," Alpha Erick says. I follow him into the house where Walter is lying on the floor, dead, covered in blood. He stands over Walter waiting for something.

"Kate, knew to get Alanis out of here; this is not going to be pretty," Alpha Erick says. I stand back, watching and waiting. What the hell is going on? All of a sudden, Walter leaps to his feet. He is hissing at Alpha Erick and making crazy sounds. He is a fucking vampire.

"What the fuck?" I scream as I stand back, trying to end of the first meal of my wife's father.

"Stay back," Alpha Erick screams at me.

"No problem, man," I say, taking a few more steps back.

"Stop," Walter says. He is trying to calm down and not eat one of us.

"I have to put you down, Walter," Alpha Erick says. Walter nods his head and then walks calmly to a chair. He sits down, jerking his body in irregular movement. He twitches and twists his body.

"They are after her," Walter says, twitching. He moves his eyes around in a nonhuman way. He rocks back and forth, fighting the vampire form, trying to take over his body.

"He and that elite whore, they want her. They were willing to kill my Jasmine to have her, but I stopped them, and Jasmine got away, at least I think she did. You have to save Jasmine and Alanis. He wants her. He wants her," Walter says, almost muddling the words.

"We will keep her safe. This is her husband, Alpha Sebastian. He will make sure Alanis is safe," Alpha Erick says, kneeling down in front of Walter.

"Put me down, Alpha. My kind has been nothing but a burden to you and your pack. Just please, save my Jasmine and protect Alanis," Walter says.

"Who was it?" Alpha Erick asks Walter.

"Conrad and Iris," Walter says. Walter moves toward Alpha Erick with his fangs out. He reaches to something at Alpha Erick's side. He grabs the stake Alpha Erick was hiding and stabs himself in the heart.

Alpha Erick moves out of the way fast. "Fuck man," I scream. This place is strange. What the hell have I gotten Alanis in, and how the hell can I help her through all of this.

Alpha Erick and I go out of the cottage. Some wolves pull up to help us. "Take Walter and burn the body," Alpha Erick says.

I look at him strangely. "He is a vampire Alpha Sebasitan. You have to burn the body. If Alanis is like Kate and Belle, then you better decide what she wants you to do if she dies. Does she want to live as a vampire, or does she want you to stake her?" Alpha Erick says.

I stand there stunned for a moment. "Alanis is a vampire?" I question him. A million questions are running through my mind.

"I do not know what her gifts are, and she will have to figure that out. The imperials are descendants of Vampires, Witches, and werewolves. Alanis might not be a vampire. My wife is a unique hybrid and so is my daughter. Your wife is an elite wolf. She has gifts like my daughter. You two will have a lot of challenges, but Kate and I got through it and we made the hard decisions early. You and Alanis need to do the same thing. Find out what gifts she has and then make decisions accordingly," Alpha Erick says.

Here I thought we were coming to find out why she can heal wolves or see death only to find out the love of my life could possibly be a vampire. This is a lot to take in at one time. I will talk to her about it tonight, first things first. Iris and Conrad have to be handled, and Jasmine needs to be located. These things are the most important right now. I have to keep Alanis safe from anyone that wants to harm her, no matter who it is.

"Alpha Sebastian," Alpha Erick hollers for me. He is talking to a group of his wolves. I walk over to see what is going on with them. "This is Jamie, and he says he saw Jasmine running through the woods a few hours ago. I am sending a few wolves to look for her going in that direction. I think you and I should go to Conrad's. He was a friend of Walters and Jasmine's. So I can ask him when the last time he saw them and see how he acts," Alpha Erick says.

"Good plan," I say. The two of us begin walking with three of Alpha Erick's warriors toward a truck.

Alpha Erick gets into the front with the driver. I get in the back with the other two men. "Sit in the middle. I do not need anything happening to you because Conrad wants your wife," Alpha Erick says.

I get in the middle between two warriors. "I do not understand why he wants my wife," I say.

Alpha Erick looks back at me. "He wants to make an elite child. You and Alanis would create an elite wolf hybrid, but two elites would create one hell of a warrior, and that is what he wants. He wants a baby with her," Alpha Erick says.

I growl so loud it scares every wolf in the truck. "If he touches Alanis, I WILL KILL HIM!" I growl.

Chapter 10

Alanis POV

Luna Kate and her daughter Belle are both in the kitchen making lunch with two she-wolves. I watch them. I wonder if Alpha Sebastian and I will have a child that is special like Belle or a child that is a wolf. Either way, I would love to have a child with Alpha Sebastion someday. That is something for later in our life. We have a lot to figure out.

It had to be difficult for Luna Kate to be pregnant and to try to figure out her wolf and her powers. Maybe that is what pushed her over the edge and caused her problems in her marriage. I want to get all of this figured out before I even think about having a child with Alpha Sebastian.

Belle comes into the living room where I am sitting, watching the two of them. She hands me a napkin with a cookie inside it. "For you," she says, sweetly with a smile. Her little curls hang down in her face.

"Come on," Luna Kate calls to her daughter. Belled leaves me alone with my cookie and my thoughts.

"We can hear you. Belle and I are linked just like you, and your child will be linked. It isn't easy sometimes. Even when I am not listening, she is a child and does not know when to mind her own business, and those thoughts pop right into my head," Luna Kate says.

I finish the cookie. "I was thinking about how hard it had to be when you were pregnant with her and learning so much about yourself," I say. I do not want her to think I was thinking badly of her or her situation. After all, she is trying to help me.

Before she can say anything, her cell phone rings. Luna Kate answers it and walks out of the living room. Belle returns. "You will be fine, Luna Alanis," Belle says.

"You think so?" I ask her.

She shakes her head. "You are like me. I know everything will be fine for both of us," Belle says.

"Good," I say.

Belle sits down beside me and finishes eating her cookie. Luna Kate comes back after a few moments. "Our husbands are going to talk to Conrad and Iris about Walter. They got a trail on Jasmine, and Alpha Erick puts some wolves on it. Hopefully, we will know something soon," Luna Kate says.

Her face says something else. Is she leaving something out? "Come on, Belle. I need you to get your lunch and go up to your room with Maggie, "Luna Kate says.

Belle shakes her head and follows her mother. Maggie, one of the she-wolves, takes Belle by the hand. "Secure the children, just in case there are any problems. Especially Belle, she might try to help if things get, bad and I want her safe. Do not let anything happen to my children," Luna Kate says.

"Yes, Luna Kate," Maggie says. She takes Belle into the kitchen to grab her lunch. Belle is fussing at Maggie as the two fades into the hallway and go up the stairs to the children's room.

"Do you know how it works as an Imperial? Do you know about being a hybrid? What I mean, do you know what happened when you die?" Luna Kate questions me.

I shake my head vigorously. "No, all of this is new to me. I have no idea about anything," I answer her.

"When an imperial wolf dies, if they are a hybrid and most of us are. I am, and you could be; we will figure that out after everything settles. Okay. When a hybrid dies, the vampire takes over. You feed and you become a vampire or you die. It is your choice, except here. In order to live here a hybrid has to die when they become a vampire," Luna Kate says.

"Wait, are you about to tell me that Walter is a vampire now?" I ask Luna Kate.

She reaches over and takes my hand. "He killed himself after he started showing vampire urges. So, he never turned; he was well on his way when he told Alpha Erick everything that happened and who did it to him," Luna Kate says.

"What did he say happened?" I ask, but I already know the answer. I know that she is about to tell me that creepy guy had something to do with this and his whore girlfriend.

"Walter told Alpha Erick that Conrad and Iris attacked them. That Jasmine got away and is running from them, but wolves are looking for her, so hopefully, they will find her first. Alpha Erick, Alpha Sebastian, and three warriors are on their way to talk to Conrad and see what he does or does not say. Trust me, and Alpha Erick will not let this go. If they are the ones that killed Walter the first time, then they will pay for what they did," Luna Kate says.

I shift around in my seat, thinking, wondering. "Luna Kate, what do they want with me?" I ask.

Luna Kate moves from beside me, obviously upset. I try to look into her mind, but she has me blocked. She paces for a moment then turns to me. "Alanis, do not panic, but Conrad wants you as his mate," Luna Kate says.

I jump to my feet. "I am married," I scream.

Luna Kate grabs me, putting her arms on me and looking into my eyes, trying to calm me. "We will handle this, I promise you," Luna Kate says.

"Why doesn't he just find another mate?" I ask.

"Because Alanis, you are special. It is more like he needs you to breed, not to be his mate. He does not want you as his equal. He wants you as someone to produce heirs for him so he can take over the imperial wolf pack," Luna Kate says.

My eyes feel as if they are going to jump out of their sockets; my heart is racing. "I do not want to be anything for him," I scream.

Chapter 11

Alpha Erick and Alpha Sebastian both arrive at my cabin. I send Iris to deal with them. She can talk to them sweetly while I leave. If both of them are occupied, this is the perfect time to take Alanis. I go out the back and shift into my wolf. I run as fast as I can across the field and deep into the woods. I can go across the creek and down to the side of the wolf territory. I can be at the Alpha's packhouse before they realize I am not at the cabin.

The wind whips through my fur as I run through the woods and make it to the clearing beside the packhouse. I stop and watch for a moment. I can smell her. I know Alanis is in there with Luna Kate. I only need for her to come outside, and I can take her away from her to be mine. I wait and wait, watching and smelling her sweet scent.

The night begins to fall as I continue to wait. Alpha Erick and Alpha Sebastian still are not back from talking with Iris. She has such beautiful gifts that work well on men, but I do not think any of her skills will work on either of them. She held Alpha Sebastian's attention for a moment today, but he is a tough one.

I could give up, or I could storm in there and grab her. Luna Kate and her daughter are the problem. If either of them goes after me, they can take me down fast. I will have to go in quietly. I know the layout of the house. I will go in the back and through the basement. Fuck it! I am going after Alanis. I want her to be mine. If I cannot have her, then I would rather be dead.

I stay in the woods and make my way to the backside of the packhouse. I can see the back windows and the basement door. Then I see her. There is Luna Alanis, my future, my love, and my future Luna. She will be the Luna of the Imperial pack when we take it over, even if she has to be my Luna from inside a cage. I will murder her, Alpha, and marry her. She will have my heirs and be my lover, no matter how I have to make it happen. Her parents promised her to me, and now, now I want someone to make good on that promise.

Luna Alanis is looking out the window of the bottom floor. That is the guest room. I can get to her. She looks so upset and maybe worried. She looks away and then goes back into her room. Maybe she is sleeping or resting. I need to grab her before Alpha Sebastian or Alpha Erick comes back. I make my move. I run across the grounds to the back of the house.

I stand under the window and then look inside the window. She is lying on the bed, resting. She is probably not asleep. I push the window open, and I move into the window slowly. I make my way to her bed and grab her quickly. She looks up at me. Her eyes grow big. I put my hand over her mouth. "If you scream, I will kill you," I say to her. She nods, okay. I take her to the window and go out of the window with her. I hold her as I run toward the woods.

Alpha Erick and Alpha Sebastian pull up in front of the packhouse. "Sebastian!" Alanis screams. Alpha Erick and Alpha Sebastian look toward us. I run faster to get as far away from the packhouse as possible.

"Let me go!" Alanis screams.

"Shut up!" I say to her. I keep running. I have to get her somewhere safe, somewhere the Alpha's cannot find her or anyone else. There are Imperials and elite wolves that do not care for Luna Kate or Alpha Erick. Those wolves will help me. They will let me hide out with my new bride.

I run for the cabin at the farthest end of the wolf property. Most wolves think it is abandoned, but it is not. There are elite wolves there, and they can help me. They will worship Alanis. Two elite wolves, Alanis and I, we will be immortalized by the elite wolves that want to break away from Alpha Erick and Luna Kate.

I run until I finally make it to the old cabin. I carry Alanis through the front door. The house looks as if it is in shambles. I drag Alanis toward the basement door. I knock on the door and wait. Alanis screams while we wait. I hate to hurt her, but she leaves me no choice. I hit her hard enough to knock her out. I cannot handle her fighting me anymore. I will have to break her in once we settle with the elite wolves.

My arms are scratched, and I have bruises from her hitting me. I hold her as unconscious body, waiting for the door to open. After about an hour, finally, an elite wolf opens the door.

"Conrad," the old elite says.

He looks at Alanis in my arms. "I have her. I took her from the Alpha. She will be my mate, and we will rise up against the wolves that oppress us," I say to the old elite wolf.

He calls down into the basement, and other elite wolves rush up to see. "It is her," several of the elite wolves are joyous seeing that I have found our lost queen. The luna that was given away by her parents.

The old elite wolf looks around and then motions for me to come into the basement. "Follow the she-wolves to a place for the two of you to rest. I will make a more permanent arrangement for you," the old elite wolf says.

"Thank you. She is not here willingly. I will need a way to contain her until I can convince her this is her correct path," I say.

The old elite wolf smiles at me. "I will bring in a cage," He says.

Chapter 12

Alpha Sebastian POV

Alpha Erick and I arrive back at the packhouse. Everything seems fine at first, other than the fact we did not speak with Conrad. We did speak with Iris. We both agreed she was hiding something and that she needed to be watched in case Conrad returns or Jasmine shows up at their cabin.

"Sebastian!" I hear screaming. It is Alanis. I look to see her and a wolf running into the woods. She is fighting as Alpha Erick and I both run toward the woods. We run through the trees, listening for her, but nothing, not another sound, is coming from her in any direction. What did he do to her to shut her up? Why must he take my wife? Breeding, I already know the answer to the question. He will rape her and make her have his pups against her will. If I do not get her back, her life will be hell. Alanis does not deserve this!

Alpha Erick and I continue to search for her. I hear someone running up behind us fast. I turn to see a white wolf. It is Luna Kate. "Which way did she go? Did you see?" Luna Kate asks.

"No, I heard her, and then she disappeared into the wood with Conrad," I growl.

"There is something you need to know. Belle saw something, and I told her not to say anything until we got back from seeing her parents. I did not want her or you to worry about her. She needed to accept her past, and damn I should have told her. She might have just left and said to hell with the elites and the imperials," Luna Kate is not making any sense right now.

"I know you wanted to help her," I say.

"I did not feel it was my place to say anything or Belle's either, but now. Things are different. She is in danger," Luna Kate says.

"Spit it out, Luna. What are you trying to say?" I ask her.

"Alanis, she is pregnant. She is not very far along, but Belle can sense the baby. She is pregnant, and now they are both in danger," Luna Kate says.

I growl loudly and begin running in all directions. I have to find my wife. I cannot let anything happen to her. If he finds out she is pregnant with my child, he might hurt her and the baby. He could kill them both.

"Alpha Sebastian," Alpha Erick calls out to me.

I take a deep breath. I am not getting anywhere by losing my mind. Other wolves are starting to come into the woods to help us look for my love, my Alanis.

"We will find her," Alpha Erick says. He looks at Luna Kate.

"We cannot involve her, Erick. It is dangerous," Luna Kate says.

"We all will protect her. We need her, or else Alanis and her baby might not make it," Alpha Erick says.

Luna Kate turns and runs back toward the house. I look at Alpha Erick. I am not sure what is going on. "She is going to bring Belle with us. Belle will be able to sense the child and Alanis since they are so much alike. We have to keep an eye on Belle. She is powerful and can be hard to handle. Trust me, and when your baby is born, you will see what I am talking about. Your life will be so different Imperial babies, especially elite children are a handful, Sebastian and Alanis she will need you," Alpha Erick says.

I nod my head. I have no idea what Alanis and I will face as parents to a child with gifts like her, but together we can face it, no matter what happens. BUT first, I have to get her home to me. That son of a bitch better not touch her in any way. I will kill him and that bitch he is with.

"Erick!" Luna Kate is running toward us. Belle is running behind her. I have never seen such a small shifter before. She looks ferocious and adorable as she runs behind her mother growling. There is another wolf, an older wolf running behind them.

We wait for Luna Kate, Belle, and the older wolf to catch up to us. A few of Erick's wolves are already searching the woods surrounding the packhouse. It should not be long until we find them.

The older wolf comes up to me. She looks me in the eyes. "I know where they are located, and I will take you there," the older wolf says.

"Who are you? And why should I trust you?" I ask her.

She looks back at Luna Kate and Alpha Erick. "I am Jasmine. I am Alanis's mother. Well, I am her birth mother. I did not raise her, and I cannot take the title, but I will help you retrieve her. But, promise me you will take her away from this place and never come back here with her. I wanted her to have a life away from this shit, but you dragged her right into it and to Conrad," Jasmine says.

"She has no idea who she is and wants answers," I say to Jasmine. I look over at Luna Kate. One thing I know for certain, unless I want Alanis to have the exact mental breakdown Luna Kate had, then I need to allow her the time to heal and learn about her past.

"She does not need to know about her past," Jasmine protests.

Luna Kate moves closer to us. She was giving us space, but she moves to butt into the conversation. "She needs to know who she is and where she came from, or she will lose her mind. I almost lost my family because I was hidden from the imperials for so long. She needs to know everything, Jasmine. Then she can make her own decisions," Luna Kate says.

"Well, we will have to disagree. She is at the old house at the edge of the wolf territory. It looks like it is abandoned, but it is not. She is in the basement with Conrad. The elite wolves have her caged and getting her ready to breed for them," Jasmine says.

"How do you know?" I growl at her.

"Because I was there when they brought her into the house. You can go into the front door, but you will need me to get you in the side door to the basement. After that, you are on your own. I am leaving this place," Jasmine says.

"You will not help rescue her? She is your daughter!" Luna Kate screams at Jasmine.

"She has not been my daughter for a very long time. I am only helping you because Conrad does not deserve her," Jasmine says.

After this woman gets us in the house to rescue Alanis, I will kill her and take joy in it.

Chapter 13

Alanis POV

I awake in a cage, again. For the second time in my life, I am confined. This time by someone who is more psychotic than the last wolf that locked me away. This one is delusional and crazy. I look around the room and see him, and he is staring at me, looking at me and wanting me. I can sense his want for me.

"We are supposed to be together, but your mother, Jasmine, she sent you away to be with Merril and his bitch. You were supposed to be my mate," Conrad growls. His wolf is fighting to take over, and I am afraid. I know that his wolf wants me. He will take my body for his. My body belongs to my husband.

"I have a mate. I belong to Alpha Sebastian. I am not your mate, Conrad. Please let me go before it is too late," I beg him.

I thought Luna Kate said he was harmless, but he is not. He is far from harmless. He looks as if he is ready to rape me and then possibly kill me. I do not think he wants me for a mate. I think he wants to own me and rule over me.

"You are mine. You were promised to me on the day you were born," Conrad hisses at me.

"I was only a child, and so were you. Conrad, my parents sent me away because they felt it was for the best. Why not let it go and find someone to love," I say to him, calmly. I am not sure if I should just tell him the truth or lie to him, but I will try this first. I am not sure I can talk any sense into him.

The door to our room opens, and an elder wolf comes into the room. He walks over to Conrad and congratulates him like I am a prize deer he shot and killed. "She is beautiful, and she will help us build a force of elite wolves to murder all of them. She is the one," the elder says.

"I will mate her soon," Conrad says.

The elder wolf walks over to my cage. He licks his lips and looks me up and down. "We want to watch," he says. He looks back at Conrad.

"What?" I scream.

"It is custom for there to be a mating ceremony for elite wolves. My wife did it, and so will you," the elder says.

"You mean rape ceremony. I will not give him my body willingly," I scream.

The elder laughs in my face. He opens my cage and walks toward me. I am not afraid of him. "You should cower beneath me, Alanis. You will serve this pack and be the queen. You will give us children until your body breaks down, but, until then, you will obey me," the elder elite wolf says.

"I will not!" I charge at him and try to get from the cage, but Conrad is at the door waiting for me. Guards begin to file into the room with us.

"Bring the chains. She does not know how to act," the elder elite wolf says.

I move to the far corner away from Conrad and the elder wolf. The two of them are both looking at me. This would be an excellent time to use my power, but I had not gotten to that with Luna Kate yet. I close my eyes and try to mind link with her.

Please help me! Luna Kate, Help ME! I scream inside my head. I need her to hear me.

"She cannot hear you while you are in here," the elder elite wolf says. The guards come into the cage and begin putting the chains on me. The chains burn my wrist and my ankles. They lock the chains in place in the corner of the cage. I cannot move.

"If you need water or food, or to even piss you will need to ask someone bitch!" the elite wolf says as he walks out of the cage. One of the guards touches my face as he leaves the cage.

"She is feisty. We may need to drug her in case she comes into her powers before she decides that it is easier to cooperate. Do not let her get to you. It is not rape. She is your mate, and it is her duty to mate with you," the elder elite wolf says.

"What is your name, wolf?" I call out to him.

"Why? You can call me your master for now," he says, laughing.

"No, I am to know your name so that when my husband kills you and Conrad, I can scream to the top of my lungs that you are dead!" I say.

The elder elite wolf opens the cage and comes back into it. He grabs me by the throat and holds it tight. I begin to gag, and I cannot breathe. "Kill me bitch.PLEASE Do it! I want you to kill me. I know that my Alpha is going to murder you, and that will send him over the edge," I say to him. I spit in his face when he lets go of my neck.

The elder elite wolf leans toward me and licks my ear. "My name is Noah. Remember it because you will be screaming fuck me, master Noah tonight in front of everyone," Noah says.

Noah slaps me across the face hard. My ears begin to ring. I look back at him, and he punches my face. He grabs my face with one hand and then rips my shirt with the other. He begins removing my clothes until I am shackled in front of him naked, and there is nothing I can do about it. I will not cry. I will not give him that satisfaction.

Noah grabs my nipples and pinches them. "I wonder how long I can pinch these until you begin to scream," Noah says. I do not say anything. I look at him as he pains me. I will not give in. I do not care if he pinches my nipples off of my body. I will not give in, and then something odd happens; the pain is gone, and I hear a voice.

"I am taking your pain, and we are coming for you. Be strong, little wolf," Luna Kate says. I cannot let him know that she mind-linked me. I roll my eyes into the back of my head and pretend to hurt still, and he finally gives up and turns loose of me.

Noah pulls me to him and kisses me. "That is my mate," Conrad protests.

"No, I think I want her to be mine," Noah says.

Noah smiles at me. He steps out of the cage, locks the cage door, and then motions for his guards. "Take him and put him somewhere. I do not care where. Just stripe him, chain him up and give him to someone. We have the breeder. We really do not need him," Noah says.

"NOOOO," Conrad protests. The guards grab him and begin pulling him out of the room. "I love you, Alanis!" he screams at me. I hope they kill him.

Noah looks at me and smiles as he leaves the room. At least I am alone now, and I know Luna Kate can hear me. I close my eyes and try to relax. The chains are burning and bruising me, but I know my Alpha is coming for me. I know I will be safe. I cannot let any of this screw with my head. I have come too far. I just need them to get here before Noah comes to try to rape me.

Chapter 14

Luna Kate is able to connect with Alanis. She begins doubling over in pain. Luna Kate screams out and then calms herself. Alpha Erick takes her hand. I know this pains him. Luna Kate lays her head back. I touch her shoulder, trying to offer my comfort.

"She is taking her pain and communicating with her," Alpha Erick says.

Luna Kate begins breathing heavier and heavier, and she opens her eyes. "We have to hurry," Luna Kate says.

"Is she in the old house like Jasmine said?" I ask her.

Tears are coming fast and frequently as Luna Kate tries to control her breathing. "Yes, thank goodness it stopped," Luna Kate says, holding her chest. She looks inside her shirt.

"He is hurting her, but it stopped," Luna Kate says. She looks at her wrist. Bruises are forming on her wrist. She checks her ankles, and they are developing bruises also. He has her tied in silver shackles.

"What is happening?" I ask.

"I am linked to her. I can feel everything she feels, hears, and sees. We are both experiencing each other's reality. If she taps into my link, she will know we are on our way to her," Luna Kate says.

"What did he do to her?" I ask.

Luna Kate looks at me. "Do not do that right now. If we hurry, it will not get that far, but you know what they want her for, we both do. Let's focus on getting to her for now," Luna Kate says.

"She is already pregnant," I say softly. "She is pregnant, and she does not even know it," I repeat myself.

"I can tell her through our mind link, but do you want that worry on her right now," Luna Kate says.

"No, I do not want that on her. I want to get her out of there before they hurt her!" I yell out.

"Come on, and we need to get going. We have twenty wolves now ready to fight. That should be enough," Alpha Erick says.

We take our wolf forms and begin to run toward the woods, with Jasmine leading the way. I do not trust her, but I have no choice right now. She knows where my love is, and for now, she is my only hope to get her back. I can smell Alanis as we run. This is the way she went with that bastard. I can smell him too. I can think of nothing except killing him. I want him dead. I want him to suffer for doing this to her. Alanis has been through enough in her young life, and now this!

We make it to the clearing, and we can see the house. It looks abandoned and almost destroyed. Everything is falling off of it. The windows appear busted, and the paint is chipping. Alpha Erick motions for a group of wolves to go into the house and another group to surround the house. Luna Kate, Alpha Erick, and I walk behind the group going into the house. Jasmine is in front of us. I keep my eyes on her. I do not trust her.

"This way," Jasmine says. She pushes past the group of wolves when we go into the house. There is a door that appears to be off its hinges and hanging in the doorway oddly. It looks like it does not belong there. Jasmine moves the door to the side, revealing another door. She hits a button, and the door opens.

"She is down there," Jasmine says.

"You first," Alpha Erick says.

Jasmine looks down into the darkness. She begins shaking her head, panicking. "They will kill me for bringing you here," Jasmine says.

Alpha Erick steps closer to her. "I said you first," he repeats himself and then moves her to the doorway. She goes down in front of us. The lights begin to come on as she descends into the darkness.

I go behind her and then Alpha Erick. Luna Kate is coming up the back with two wolves, Leaving one wolf at the door and wolves surrounding the house.

"Send in the next group in about twenty minutes," Alpha Erick call up to the wolf standing at the door.

"Yes, Alpha," he says.

At least we will have more wolves coming to help us if something goes wrong. Jasmine walks ahead of me and comes to another door. She knocks on the door, and we wait. Alpha Erick must have a bad feeling. He pushes her out of the way and kicks in the door. Behind the door is another house. It is like the old house leads to a much bigger house that is underground.

"They know we are here," Jasmine says.

"I know," Alpha Erick says.

He goes into the opening of the underground house. I follow him. Several wolves are approaching us as we make our way through the opening.

"Who are you?" One of the wolves calls out to him.

"Alpha Erick, and you have something that belongs to Alpha Sebastian. We want her back or we will kill everyone in this place," Alpha Erick demands.

"What do we have?" the wolf asks.

I step forward. "My wife," I growl.

The two wolves look at each other. "The breeder is a Luna," one of the wolves says.

"Take me to my wife!" I growl. The two wolves are shaking as I growl at them.

Luna Kate steps forward glowing. "My best advice to you would be to give me my wife before Luna Kate melts your brain," I say.

Luna Kate grabs one of them. She is glowing, and after a moment, he is glowing. It scares the hell out of me to think this is one of the powers Alanis has in her toolbox.

"She is in the basement with Noah. He wants to mate her and breed her tonight in a breeding ceremony," the other wolf says. After watching his friend glow, he becomes so frightened that he spills everything and then passes out on the floor.

"Well, that cannot be his guards," Alpha Erick says, looking at the young wolf lying on the floor.

"No, no way it is," I say.

Luna Kate holds the glowing wolf in her hands. "Show me the basement," she says. He points toward the end of the hallway.

"Take me to her," Luna Kate says. She releases the wolf, and we follow him to the end of the hall. He opens the door with a key, and steps lead into a basement behind the door. I thought we were already underground. There are no windows, and everything is so dark. How far under are we going?

"Lead the way," Luna Kate says.

We descend into the basement to rescue my love. As we get to the bottom of the steps, blood begins coming out of Luna Kate's nose. "Fuck!" Luna Kate screams.

Alpha Erick rushes to her side. "What is happening?" I ask her.

"He is beating her," Luna Kate says.

"HELP ME!" Alanis screams out.

We are close, so very close to my love.

Chapter 15

Alanis POV

"Please stop!" I scream out, crying and begging. I just want it to stop. Luna Kate is taking some of the pain, but I am breaking. I cannot take much more.

Noah strikes me across the face. "Give in to me, Alanis. Say it! Say you will be mine. Release Alpha Sebastian as your mate and become mine," Noah says, hitting me again.

Blood is streaming down my face. I look at him, spit out my blood, and growl as loud as I can. I feel the power coming from within me, but the shackles and the silver are holding me back. "HELP ME!" I scream out to anyone that is listening.

We are close, I hear in my mind. Luna Kate is coming, and she has my sweet Alpha with her. They will save me. Noah puts his hands around my throat and begins shocking me. "Say it! Alanis or I will just take it. You can be my mater, or you can be my breeder. I am giving you a choice!" Noah screams at me.

"Take it. Go ahead, take it from me," I cry out.

"I will, my little bitch!" Noah says. He unbuckles his pants and stands in front of me erect. I begin to cry out! I cannot stand the thought of him touching me.

"No, NO NO! Please do not do this! Please Stop!" I scream. Noah presses against me. I can feel him so close to me. He is at my entrance. He kisses my neck and then moves down my body. His harness rubs against my leg as he kisses me.

"I like it when you scream; it makes me hard," Noah says.

"Please don't do this. I have a mate," I beg him.

His hand makes contact with my pussy. He grabs me hard. I gasp. He moves his hand up and down. "Has Luna Kate told you that when you suffer, you become stronger. I am going to make you suffer, Alanis.

You will be so powerful when I am done with you. You will truly be an elite wolf after I finish with you," Noah says.

"HELP ME!" I scream

"I like that; scream again!" Noah laughs in my face. His tongue slides into my mouth, and he licks my face. "TASTY!" he moans.

The door opens to the room. Alpha Sebastian and Erick came into the room with Lune Kate. Alpha Sebastian rushes to me, but Noah is prepared. He puts a knife to my throat.

"I will slice her throat and gut this bitch!" he screams at my sweet Alpha.

"Let her go, Noah," Alpha Erick says.

"No. She is mine now. She belongs with her own kind. She needs to be here just the way it was intended for her to be. She was supposed to be mated to the elite wolves, and we want what is ours back. I want to make her scream my name. You can watch me mark her as mine!" he says so arrogantly.

"She is with child, you idiot!" Luna Kate says.

Noah kisses my ear. "I am right there. Are you ready? I am going to fuck you while he watches, and then I am going to cut that half-breed wolf out of your body," Noah says.

"Sebastian!" I scream out!

Wolves come into the small room. They begin fighting. I bite at Noah and try to get away from him, but I cannot. I cannot get away from him. He is going to take me. Alpha Sebastian moves fast and puts his hand between me and the knife. Noah stabs my sweet Alpha. Luna Kate rushes to me while Alpha Erick takes care of the elite wolves coming into the room. She and Alpha Sebastian fight off Noah and are able to release me from the shackles. Everything is happening so fast.

I feel myself finally released from the last shackle. I take a deep breath. I run for Alpha Sebastian. I take his hand and heal him quickly. Noah looks surprised when I heal Alpha Sebastian.

"You have a unique gift," he says. Luna Kate holds him. I pick the knife up from the ground.

"NO, ALANIS!" Alpha Erick screams out.

"Don't!" Luna Kate screams, but it is too late. I jump onto off Noah and begin stabbing him. I cannot stop. I strike him over and over. I feel something so raw and something so free. I am free, and I am powerful. His blood is all over me. I throw down the knife and begin to walk out of the room. I walk past Alpha Sebastian and Alpha Erick.

Luna Kate follows me. "Alanis," she calls out to me.

I turn to look at her. "I feel different," I say to her. I do feel odd. I feel like I have worlds coursing through my veins. I am full of Imperial and Elite energy.

Alpha Sebastian and Alpha Erick come to the doorway. The three of them follow me as we walk down the hall and then to the steps to go up and out of the house. When we get to the top step, there is a small doorway. I look over to see Conrad. He is shackled and hanging. I move my hand and open the door.

I go into the room where he is being held. "Conrad," I say softly.

"Alanis, you found your power. You look beautiful," Conrad says to me.

"Thank you," I say. I reach up and remove his shackles one at a time.

"What are you doing?" Conrad asks.

"I am freeing you," I answer him. Alpha Sebastian and Alpha Erick are watching me.

"Help me get him out of here," I ask Luna Kate.

"Why?" she asks me.

"They used him and manipulated him. He does not deserve this," I say.

Conrad falls onto me, and I hold him. I lean into him and kiss his lips, healing him. He looks into my eyes. "Will you be my mate now?" he asks me.

"No, I am going to free you now, Conrad," I say to him.

Conrad smiles. I reach into his chest and pull out his heart. He drops to the floor. I walk away. I am an elite wolf now, and I will be respected!

Chapter 16

She drops him, taking his heart and then walking away like it is nothing. She is falling into that dark place where her power is the strongest. I wanted to guide her so she could avoid the darkness, but whatever Noah did to her, it pushed her into that place. I know that darkness all too well. It is vengeful, and it pulls you into a dark cloud where nothing is as it seems. You think everyone is against you, but in reality, the only person against you is yourself.

"What now?" Alpha Sebastian asks me.

I look to Alpha Erick. He will have to help me with this. It will be difficult for both him and me, but we have to do this.

"For now, we have to take care of her and let her know that she is loved. I will help guide her from the darkness, but we have to hurry. The only person that was able to pull me out of the darkness was Erick. Alpha Sebastian, you will have to endure whatever she throws at you and help her. Never stop loving her, and she will pull herself out of the darkness," I say.

"There is nothing she could do that would make me not love her," Alpha Sebastian says.

Alpha Erick looks pained. I can tell he is thinking about the pain I caused him. "No, but she can push you very close to losing your mind," he says. I know he is being honest. I almost caused us to lose our family. I take the blame for all of that. I ran with Belle, I accused him of cheating on me, I made his life hell, yet he still loved me and worked until he pulled me from the darkness. I know Alpha Sebastian can do the same.

Luna Alanis is lucky to have him. We go up the stairs and out into the main floor of the crumbling house. I expect there to be guards or wolves or someone coming for us after killing Noah and Conrad, but there is nothing but quiet. The wolves from our pack are waiting for us when we come up.

"What is going on?" I ask Alpha Erick. He goes to his wolves and talks to them, leaving Alpha Sebastian and me behind. I give him the space he needs to handle his business. He calls out to Alpha Sebastian, and the two take their wolf forms and run toward the woods. I step out of the crumbling house to return to the packhouse with the security team left behind, and that is when I see her, Jasmine.

Jasmine is dead. Luna Alanis ripped her heart from her body and crushed her. She is in full rage mode, and the darkness has her. My biggest fear in all of this is that my mother, the one who caused so much of the pain between the wolves of the Imperial pack and the vampire she mated with, that she Rainwater is pulling at Luna Alanis and guiding her into a darkness just like mine.

I take my wolf form and begin running toward the house. Belle, my mind goes to Belle. I try to connect with her, but she is not listening to me. That is not like her. Belle listens to everything. It is hard to have a moment when she is not in my mind. There is no way Luna Alanis would hurt my child, but what if Belle is telling her about the child she is carrying inside her? Will Alanis respond to Belle and listen to her when she tells her how difficult her pregnancy will be and how she will need vampire blood even to survive what is to come? I cannot leave this burden on Belle.

I run toward the packhouse as fast as I can. I think of nothing but Belle as I run, hoping she will know that I am coming for her. Even if she cannot respond, she will know that mommy is coming. When I get to the edge of the treeline, I see Luna Alanis. She is standing there with Belle, and she seems to be calm. I walk slowly to her. Alpha Erick and Alpha Sebastian are both close by and watching.

"Belle," I call out to her.

"Not now, mommy," she says. I notice the glowing light coming from Belle. She has Luna Alanis and is protecting her from the darkness.

"Is she okay?" I ask Belle.

"Yes, Mommy," Belle answers me. That is enough for me. I trust Belle. I join Alpha Erick and Alpha Sebastian.

"You two left me," I say.

Alpha Erick puts his arm around me. "I was afraid she might hurt the children. I had to get to them fast. I am sorry, my love," Alpha Erick says.

"She would never hurt a child," Alpha Sebastian says.

"Luna Alanis would never hurt a child, but the darkness in her could kill us all," I say to him.

"How do we save her?" Alpha Sebastian asks me.

"That is something Alpha Erick will have to help you with. He pulled me out. Trust me, I was a lot worse and left a lot of destruction in my path," I say.

I walk toward Belle to keep an eye on her and Luna Alanis. I want Alpha Erick and Alpha Sebastian to have time to talk. Belle may need my help. She begins walking with Luna Alanis toward the packhouse.

"Where are you going?" I ask Belle.

"She has to rest. I am going to put her into a deep sleep for now while you figure out how to help her," Belle says.

She is right. If we can force Alanis to sleep just for now, then we can figure out how to help her. I need to go into her mind and help her work through whatever Noah did to her, and then we can fight the darkness together.

Chapter 17

Alanis POV

I walk back to the cottage with Belle. She holds my hand tries to give me some sort of peace. I feel havoc racing through my body, and I am not sure how to deal with any of it. It is a strange power that seems to be taking me over.

"Do not worry, Alanis. Mommy and daddy can help you. Especially mommy. Mommy knows how to help you," Belle says.

I let Belle lead me into the bedroom. "Get comfortable," she says. I lay on the bed, and I close my eyes. I feel her touch my stomach.

"Are you happy about your babies?" Belle asks me. I open my eyes and look at her.

"babies?" I question her.

She nods her head. "Yes, there are two," she says.

"Two?" I question her again. I touch my stomach and close my eyes.

"You can feel them, can't you. Feel their heartbeats," Belle says. I listen for the sounds of their heartbeats. Boom BoomBoom and it comes in an echo. Shit, there are two babies. I wonder what Alpha Sebastian will think of two babies and a crazy Luna.

"He is happy," Belle says, answering my questions that I do not speak out loud.

"Thanks," I say. I lay down back with my hand on my stomach. Belle is watching over me.

"You need to sleep and try to find yourself, Alanis. You seem okay now, but the darkness it will come in waves, and it is scary. I can help you sleep. Mommy can meet you in your mind and help you through everything so that you do not lose yourself," Belle says.

"Help me to rest, Belle, please," I say to her. She touches my forehead, and I fall into a deep sleep.

"Alanis," I hear someone calling out to me. I look to see Luna Kate, and she is with me. She walks toward me, and we are surrounded by a white light.

"What is happening?" I ask her.

"We are inside your mind," Luna Kate says.

It is strange to think that someone waltzed into my brain and is having a conversation with me. I wonder what else I can do or what else might happen to me as I take this journey into the unknown.

"Are you afraid?" Luna Kate asks me.

I look around at the beautiful images inside my mind. "No, I am happy and content," I say.

Luna Kate touches my arm. It feels strange when she touches me. "You can stay here with me," she says. I look into her eyes and see the darkness. I see something evil, something that is not Luna Kate. I hear someone else calling out to me. I listen, but this thing in front of me, pretending to be Luna Kate, is holding on to me.

"You will stay with me, Alanis. I told you that you are mine," the darkness in front of me growls at me.

"Let go of me!" I scream.

I run as hard as I can away from the darkness. I can hear Belle, Luna Kate, and Alpha Sebastian screaming for me. I can feel my body shaking. What the hell is going on with me?

"She is coming to us; grab her Belle," I hear Luna Kate saying. The darkness is behind me. He is running toward me, pulling me back to him.

"HELP ME!" I scream out, but everything goes quiet in my head. I listen for the heartbeats of my babies. I can hear their heartbeats. I am still alive. I take a deep breath and try to figure out how to get out of my mind.

"Wake up," I hear a voice call to me.

I am trying to wake up, but nothing is happening. I cannot get out of my own head. I feel a strong sense of something. It is almost like a warm embrace and love. It feels like love.

"I love you, Alanis," Alpha Sebastian says. I feel his hand on my hand. I feel his kiss on my lips.

"Come back to me," Alpha Sebastian pleads with me. I am trying. I am trapped in my mind, and I cannot get out.

I hear the roaring of the darkness coming for me. "Come to me," the darkness calls to me. I look to see Conrad. "You were promised to me, bitch!" he calls out to me. I try to run, but it is of no use. I cannot move.

"ALANIS!" I hear Alpha Sebastian call out to me.

I open my eyes, and Alpha Sebastian is with me, crying, holding my hand. Luna Kate and Belle are with me. "What happened? Am I out of my mind?" I ask the three of them.

I look around the room and realize I am back home. We left and came home. How did I get here? My heart begins to race. I look down to realize that my stomach has grown.

"How long was I asleep?" I ask.

Alpha Sebastian and Luna Kate both look at me and hold back, answering. "Seven months," Belle says. She blurts it out. She sits down beside me.

"What the fuck happened?" I ask.

Belle opens her mouth to start to spill everything, but Luna Kate quickly covers her mouth. "Belle go in the kitchen and find a snack," Luna Kate says to her daughter sternly.

"Yes, mommy," Belle says. When Belle gets to the bedroom door, she looks back at me. "The darkness wants you and your babies," she says and then leaves the room.

I touch my stomach that has grown leaps and bounds while I have been in a deep sleep. "Am I okay, now?" I ask.

"We think so. Belle and I worked to put up a protection around you and your babies, but it worked so well that you fell into a deep sleep, and then when we brought you out of the darkness, well, it found you, but I was able to put the protection around you again, this time without knocking you out for seven months," Luna Kate says.

"Now what?" I ask her.

"Now, we have our babies and try to live for now. We will not know if the babies are in any danger until they start shifting or showing any signs of powers," Alpha Sebastian says.

Luna Kate laughs. "Belle has spent a lot of time educating Alpha Sebastian on Imperials and Elite wolves," Luna Kate says.

"I see. Can I have a moment with my husband?" I ask Luna Kate.

Luna Kate leaves the room, leaving me alone with Alpha Sebastian. I look at him as he walks to the bed. He sits at the bedside and takes my hand. I look into his eyes. "Who are you, and where is my husband?" I demand.

He smiles, and I see the darkness in him. "Send them away, and I will not harm your precious Alpha," the darkness says.

Chapter 18

Luna Alanis POV

The darkness stares at me through Alpha Sebastian's eyes. Is he still in there? I try to reach Alpha Sebastian through our mate bond, but there is nothing. I cannot feel him at all. I am afraid for him. I will cooperate with the darkness. "Send them away now, or I will kill your precious love," the darkness says, he hisses at me. I am petrified.

"Send them in to me," I say to him. He smiles at me. For a moment his eyes shift to solid black, and it sends a shiver down my spine looking at him. I do not think Alpha Sebastian is still in there.

"I will be right back my love," the darkness says.

He goes into the front part of the house and talks with Luna Kate and little Belle. It is almost twenty minutes before the two come into my bedroom to talk to me. Belle looks at me as if she knows what is going on, but Luna Kate looks so confused.

"Are you okay? We are fine to stay until the baby comes. Alpha Erick will not mind at all," Luna Kate says.

I shake my head, trying not to look at the darkness or think anything. I hope that little Belle can feel what is going on with me. I cannot risk her life as the madness and darkness that is in the room sits with us, watching over me. Luna Kate stares into my eyes as if to stare right through me. She looks back to Alpha Sebastian or the darkness disguised as Alpha Sebastian.

"Alpha Sebastian, would you mind bringing me my tea from the kitchen. I would like to drink it before I leave and I made enough for the three of us," Luna Kate says.

The darkness smiles. "Sure, I would be happy to do that for you Luna Kate," he says. When he leaves, Luna Kate says nothing we sit in silence. I cannot hear her mind or Belle's they both have me blocked out. Maybe they know he can hear me.

Alpha Sebastian comes back with the tea on a tray. The three of us begin drinking our tea. As soon as I get half of the tea down, I can hear Luna Kate in my head. "I know that is not Alpha Sebastian. He cannot hear you when you are drinking this tea. I will make more before I leave and I will be back with an army to free you," Luna Kate says.

"I am going to miss you both," I say out loud, so that the darkness does not get suspicious of our silence. He watches us so close. Belle keeps looking back to him. He is so close to her. I can see it is making her uncomfortable, but she keeps smiling at him. To be so small she is so powerful. Does he realize who he is messing with? Belle will have him dead by sundown at the rate he is going.

"I will put you on some tea and then Belle and I will be on our way. If you or Alpha Sebastian needs us for anything, just call me. I will be here to help. All of us will be," Luna Kate says.

I know what she means. She is going back to get Alpha Erick and they are going to bring hell on earth to this dark being that is trying to keep me and my child. "Thank you for everything," I say to her.

She holds my hand for a moment. I can sense some fear, but nothing compared to what is coming off of Belle. Little Belle seems to be radiating so much fear that it is almost impossible to ignore it.

"See you soon. We can see ourselves out," Luna Kate says as she takes Little Belle's hand and leads her out the door.

"Bye Alpha Sebastian," Belle says to the darkness and then she looks at me. She smiles and blows me a kiss.

The darkness sits beside me on the bed. I can hear Luna Kate and Little Belle making tea for me before they leave. The darkness touches my face, and I pull away from him. He touches my growing belly. "My child will be here soon, Luna Alanis and this baby is spectacular. Can you feel the energy coming from your womb? Some elite wolves die in childbirth because of their child being so strong. But do not worry your pretty little head much. I will raise this baby to be a fierce warrior. We do not need you after he is born," the darkness says.

I open my mouth to scream, but nothing comes out. I begin to cry, which only seems to be enjoyed by the darkness. "Your friends are leaving. I plan to send all of your she wolves away today and it will be just you and me. This baby will be mine tonight," the darkness says.

"It is not time yet," I say to the darkness. He stands up and begins to laugh as if to taunt me and my stupid way of thinking.

"Luna Alanis, you are going to die in childbirth. I plan to keep this nice body as my own and I will raise this baby without you. I have all of your precious Alpha's memories, I can run this pack and raise this child. I do not need you," the darkness says.

"I can give you more children. Don't you want an army?" I ask the darkness. I need to buy time so Luna Kate and Alpha Erick can get back here to save Alpha Sebastian, and our baby. He can kill me, but our child has to live.

"I do, but not yet. This child can build an army for me. He can take she wolves and plant elite wolves in them, soon we will take over the world and your son will be the Alpha King of all of the wolf packs. Best part is he will call me daddy and he will worship me. I will control the Alpha King," the darkness responds.

I open my mouth to scream and again nothing comes out. "SHHH, rest up. Your son is coming soon. Sleep," the darkness says. Everything fades to darkness. I am in hell.

Chapter 19

I leave Luna Alanis behind, taking Belle and going home. Neither one of us want to leave her, but we need help to fight the dark enemy. Alanis can defeat him herself with the help of Belle, but we need the dark one occupied, and we have to ensure Alpha Sebastian's safety.

Belle and I get into our truck, and I take one last look at the house. I can feel her pain. As much as her pain hurts me, I can only imagine the way Belle feels right now. This ordeal with Alanis must be excruciating for her. The way Belle feels what is going on with other wolves is sometimes a burden for her and terrifying for me.

I drive away slowly, but when we get out of sight, I kick it into high gear and roll out of the wolf territory heading home as fast as possible. We make it to the interstate within the hour. Luna Alanis and Alpha Sebastian's pack is further away from the world than our pack. That is one reason we have to act fast. No one will know that Alanis is captive for a long time unless we help her.

Belle reaches over and takes my hand. I look down at her sweet face. "We will save her, Belle," I say to her.

Belle is distraught. "We have to save her and the little boy. He is my destiny," Belle says. What the hell does she mean by that. Her destiny, will they be friends? She cannot know who her mate is already, or does she? I cannot process all of this right now.

I grab my cell phone from the seat between Belle and me. I scroll down to Erick's number and hit call. It rings for only a moment, but it feels like forever.

"How is she?" Alpha Erick asks.

I can feel a lump in my throat, and I want to scream out how much all of this hurts me. Not just that Luna Alanis is in trouble, but that this could happen to our daughter. "The darkness has Alpha Sebastian, and we need an army. I left with Belle. I told the darkness that I was going home, but I am not. I am going to stop and get a hotel. Belle and I will wait for you. Bring an army of warriors. Belle can help Luna Alanis and Alpha Sebastian, but she needs strong men to hold the dark one down while she works on him. Luna Alanis and Belle can take the darkness out completely, but we need warriors," I say all in one breath and trying not to cry. I realize that I am crying and that I am having a panic attack. I take another deep breath. Just breathe, breathe, air in air out, calm down, Kate, I keep trying to bring myself down, but nothing is working. Why am I freaking out so badly?

"Where are you now?" Alpha Erick asks me.

"We are almost to Shiloah Town," I answer him.

"Stop in the next town and get a hotel. I will gather everyone and be there by nightfall. Get something off the highway, not too close but not too far away. I do not want you seen, but I do not want you in danger either," Alpha Erick says.

"I love you," I say.

"I love you too," Alpha Erick responds. I end the call and lay my cell phone down between Belle and me. She is not upset. I thought she would be going out of her mind, but she is calm.

"Everything will be fine; the darkness will fall," Belle says. It is cryptic and odd. The voice almost seems not to be hers. She looks at me, and her eyes flash a dark green at me.

I try to ignore what is going on with my child, but it is hard. Something or some wolf is communicating with her. Hopefully, it is someone that wants to help and not cause us harm. Oh, Belle, I never wanted this life for you. There are no guarantees in our life. It is always something. All I want is peace for Belle and her future. Maybe she and the child Alanis carries can bring the Elite Wolf Breed peace. My Belle can do anything and be anything that I know for sure. I do hate that imposed on her all of this crazy. No, I don't believe that it is my fault. It is my mother's fault.

We cross over into the next town after Shiloh Town. I pull off the interstate and go to a hotel toward the end of the road. It is back off the road but still close enough; if anything went wrong or someone came looking for us, we could get help. I do not want to raise a lot of suspicions when a lot of warriors roll into this little town, either. I do not need anyone letting the dark one know that Alpha Erick is planning to attack him and heading that way. We have to be sneaky and stealthy in our movements right now.

Belle and I get out of the truck and go into the hotel to get a room. For some reason, I feel odd, and she looks strange. "Are you okay?" I ask her.

"No, I am not. I need to rest. I have work to do soon," she says. Belle passes out as soon as the words escape her mouth. I grab her before she can hit the ground.

I carry her into the hotel lobby and get a room for us. "She is exhausted, long trip," I tell the clerk as she hands me the room key.

I take Belle to the elevator, and we go up to the second floor. I carry her to the room, unlock the door and carry her in; once inside, I lay her on the bed. She is completely out of it. I lay down beside her while she sleeps. I text Alpha Erick to let him know where we are, and then I hesitate to tell him about Belle.

"Erick," I say softly after I tell him where we are.

"What is wrong?" he asks.

I look down at Belle. "It is Belle. How quickly can you get here?" I ask him.

"Faster than you think," he says. Alpha Erick hangs up the phone. I cuddle my daughter.

Chapter 20

Luna Kate POV

I awake to the sound of someone coming into my room. I jump out of the bed and begin to shift into my wolf. Whoever is after my baby and me will die right here and now. I have been through enough, and no one is going to come in here and take her, not now or ever. I run toward the noise at the entrance to our room. I growl into the darkness when a figure steps out into the light and holds up his hand. "It is me, Kate. I did not mean to scare you," Alpha Erick calls out to me before I jump onto him.

I run to him, falling into his arms. "You did scare me. You completely freaked me out. Belle is still out of it. She said she needed rest and that she had work to do. Then she went to sleep. I want her to wake up. I am so worried," I say, sobbing into Alpha Erick's chest.

He rubs my back and holds me close to him. He kisses my forehead and then lets go of me. He goes to the bed and kneels down beside the bed to get a good look at little Belle. He moves her long hair out of her face, she smiles. She is still out of it, but she smiles at her father. Their bond is so special. I cannot believe the way he loves all of our children, but this bond is deep. He would kill for her. Actually, he has destroyed people for her. He would choose her over me any day of the week, and I am okay with that.

"Do you think the darkness did this to her or what?" Alpha Erick asks me.

I move closer to them, shaking my head. "I have no idea what is going on, Erick. I only know she is scaring the hell out of me. I need her to wake up," I say. I am shaking, and my words are broken as I speak. I want to take her home and protect her from all of this. She is just a child.

Her eyes open all at once, and she springs forward, putting her arms around him. "Daddy, we have work to do. We have to get the dark man out of Alpha Sebastian, and we have to protect Alanis and her son," she says.

Alpha Erick looks at me, but I have no explanation. I cannot answer the questions burning in his head. Only Belle can, and right now, she is leading us but not giving any real reasons for anything. All we can do is follow along and do what she asks of us. She bounces out of the bed as if she was just napping and now ready to play. She looks up at me and winks. Why is she being so cryptic?

I look at her as she passes me and then back to Alpha Erick. I slap my hands on my thighs in exasperation from the situation. "I have no idea what is going on. I cannot even hear her thoughts right now," I say.

"Can you hear Alanis?" Alpha Erick asks me.

I shake my head, and tears begin rolling down my face. "No, I am so fucking emotional I can barely cope," I say.

Alpha Erick takes my hand and holds me for a moment. "Come on. Everyone is waiting for us. We need the cover of the dark to save Alpha Sebastian and Luna Alanis. I have enough wolves here to take care of this problem quickly," Alpha Erick says.

I follow him out of the room, grabbing my cell and keys as we go out of the room. Belle is standing in the hall waiting for us. "Come on," she says. She is in a hurry and on a mission. She knows what is happening, and she knows what she has to do. I can see it.

Something weird begins to happen to me as we go down the elevator to the hotel lobby. "I do not feel well," I say.

Belle touches my face. "I need to borrow some of your power, but you will be fine," Belle says. That is why I cannot hear her in my head, our link is interrupted, and why she was asleep for so long, she was taking power from me to help Luna Alanis defeat the darkness. Luna Alanis is strong like Belle, and with a little extra juice from me, this will end well for us, not for the dark one but for us. I just hope it does not hurt me.

We get off the elevator and meet the warriors waiting for us. Belle sticks to her father. She needs him and his team right now more than me. There are times when I have to step back and let Belle just be Belle, and this is one of those times. We need her gifts to save Alpha Sebastian, Luna Alanis, and her baby. Right now, she needs my powers, but she needs Luna Alanis and her father to help her get the work done. I am entirely okay with that, as long as she is not hurt. Belle is my first priority.

"Luna Kate, take Errol, Fin, and Jack with you," Alpha Erick says.

I tilt my head as he gives the order. "And Belle?" I ask.

He picks her up and carries her on his hip. "She is coming with Ram and me. I will not let anything happen to her, I promise," Alpha Erick says.

"Take care of my baby," I say. I walk toward the truck. I can feel the pain welling up inside me and realize I can feel Luna Alanis and Little Belle again. I look back at her. She did take some power from me, but she gave me what I needed to keep an eye on her and Luna Alanis. I breathe deep and with relief. She knows what she is doing. Everything will be fine.

I get into the truck. Jack gets into the cab with me, and the other two get into the bed of the truck. "Ready?" I ask Jack.

"As I ever will be," he says. Jack knows a lot about the elite wolves and how this could go down. I am sure that is why Alpha Erick brought him along.

I pull out onto the highway, and we begin our caravan to Luna Alanis.

Chapter 21

I feel all alone. I see someone that looks like Alpha Sebastian, but it is not him. It is a dark force here to destroy me and take my baby. I lay my hand across my stomach and try to remain calm. I know Luna Kate will be back with an army to save me, but I am not sure how soon or when she will be back for me. I cannot take much more. The mental abuse from the dark one is killing my spirit. He keeps telling me that I will die alone and afraid while he raises my son. So, where is my Alpha? Did he kill him, or is he still there? I need to know my husband and child will survive this even if I do not survive.

"Who is there?" I ask as the door creeps open. A woman comes into the room with me. She has short black hair and looks like she is possessed by darkness. She bares her fangs at me and then growls. What the hell is she? Vampire? Werewolf? Both? I scream out as she comes closer to me, but nothing escapes my mouth. I begin crying. It is the only thing I can do.

"SSShhhh, no need for all of that crying. It is a joyous day. We are going to have a baby," she says. Her voice is demonic, and she makes my skin crawl. She pulls up my shirt, looks at my stomach, then touches my stomach, grabbing and pulling me. It is painful, but I do not move; I cannot move.

Another woman comes into the room, and then the darkness comes into the room. "We are getting her ready," the first woman says.

"Hurry, I think someone is coming to try to save her. Get that baby out of her now. We have to get the baby and get out of her. Do not worry about her; just make sure the baby survives," the dark one says.

"One baby cut out of one mother coming right up quickly," the woman says. If they cut the baby out of me, I will die. There is no surviving that. I know that is their plan they want me to die. They do not need me, only the child I carry.

Several women come into the room now. I try to get out of the bed. Maybe I could fight them off; where are my powers when I need them. I reach within myself and try to find something inside me to push them away from me. A spark like energy begins to manifest within me, and I feel strong again. Whatever he is doing to keep me under his control is losing its hold on me. "Back off my baby and me, bitch!" I scream.

The women closest to the door begin backing away from me, but the one that came into the room first keeps moving toward me. "No, that baby is mine. I need it for my master," she says. She starts moving closer to me. She grabs my shoulder and begins trying to force me back to the bed. I scream out, and this time, a loud scream escapes my mouth.

I place my hand on her chest and push. A ball of light and energy comes out of my hand and pushes her toward the wall. The black haired bitch hits the wall hard and then slides down the wall. She is out cold, and I turn my attention to the women in the room with me.

"Are you going to try to take my baby, or do you want to live to see another day?" I growl at them. The women run over themselves, trying to escape the room and me. I begin howling out for help, hoping someone will come to help me. I hear the front door crash open. Someone has come for me.

"Luna Alanis," I hear a faint sound, someone calling my name.

"Help me," I scream out. I listen inside my mind as things are starting to come to me. The energy, the powers, everything is building inside me. I touch my stomach to let the little one growing inside me know that we are going to be okay.

It sounds like my house is being destroyed. "Luna Alanis," the voice calls out to me again. Where is it coming from? Is it in the house or in my mind? I go to the door and open it. There are wolves everywhere fighting. I know we need to fight the dark one, but they cannot kill Alpha Sebastian.

I rush into the middle of the fighting. "STOP!" I scream out. Everyone stops. It is like time stops, and the only person who is with me is Belle and the dark one. Belle rushes to my side and takes my hand.

"We can remove him from Alpha Sebastian. It will hurt, but it will not harm Alpha Sebastian. Are you ready?" she asks me as she squeezes my hand.

"Yes, we have to save him," I say. We close our eyes and join our energies. I can feel her and Luna Kate as we push the light out of us and into Alpha Sebastian. The dark one rushes toward us to try to stop us. When he is almost to us, we release all of our powers into Alpha Sebastian. The dark one and Alpha Sebastian separate, becoming two individual beings.

Alpha Sebastian is stunned for a moment. "FIGHT!" I yell. All of the wolves seem to come alive and are ready to fight again. Alpha Sebastian runs to me, puts his arms around me, and holds me. I let go of Belle's hand as Alpha Erick picks her up. The dark one is still in the room.

"Now what?" Alpha Erick asks.

"Now we kill it," Luna Kate says. She pulls her power from within her and hits the dark one with a mighty blow. He falls to the ground and is struggling. I thought she was not as powerful as Belle and I, then I realize she is as powerful, but her power comes from a darker place inside her, and she refuses to use it. She is only using her power to ensure my baby is safe from this darkness.

"Die, you bastard," Luna Kate yells out.

The dark one begins to scream. Luna Kate's eyes are turning black as she battles the dark one. "Fuck, she is going too far. She will die to if she does not stop," Alpha Erick says.

The room becomes a force of nature as Luna Kate destroys the dark one. If she does not return to herself, it will be my fault. I run to her to help her. "Do not touch her," Alpha Sebastian yells at me.

I take Luna Kate's hand. Maybe I can help her. Little Belle struggles to get away from Alpha Erick. He finally has no choice but to let her join us. She takes my hand and her mother's hand. We form a circle and keep pushing to destroy the dark one. When the room seems almost to explode, then the dark screams out and vanishes into the floor. Luna Kate falls to the floor letting go of my hand and Little Belle.

"Mommy," Belle calls out to her mother.

Alpha Erick rushes to her. Alpha Sebastian puts his arms around me. "That scared the hell out of me," he says.

"I know, but it probably saved her life, and we owe her," I say.

"Let's go to one of the cabins; this place is destroyed. It would be best if you rested after all of this," Alpha Sebastian says.

"What about Luna Kate and Alpha Erick?" I ask.

"I will have one of the Beta's make sure they are comfortable in a guest cabin, okay," Alpha Sebastian says.

I fall into his arms. "I am unsteady. You are going to have to help me," I say. He picks me up and carries me. As we go out of the destroyed house, a pain hits me, and then a flood of water comes from me.

"Alpha Sebastian, I think the baby is coming," I say.

Chapter 22

Luna Alanis POV

Alpha Sebastian carries me to the cabin closest to our now destroyed home. "It hurts, it hurts so much, please hurry," I cry out.

He takes me into the first room and lays me on the bed. "What do I need to do?" he asks. Like I know, I have never had a baby before, and I have no idea what is happening. All I know is I am wet with water, and I am sure my water broke. I also know that the pain coming from my stomach is labor pain.

"I need Luna Kate, please get her," I say.

We are alone, and I can tell he does not want to leave me. He stands for a moment holding my hand, waiting to see if anyone follows us, but no one comes into the room.

"Go, Sebastian, I will be fine, but please hurry," I say to him. He leans down and kisses my forehead, then runs out of the cabin to get Luna Kate.

A sharp pain hits me, and I scream out in agony. I knew this would be painful, but I did not think it would happen this way. I thought I would be with the pack doctor and have drugs. I search for Luna Kate in my mind, but I cannot hear her. What if she is hurt? Please let her be okay.

The door to the cabin comes open fast, and Alpha Sebastian races back to me. He comes to my side. "Where is she?" I ask him.

"She is coming. It will be a few minutes, she is a little weak, but Belle is healing her," Alpha Sebastian says.

I shake my head. "If she is not weak, then we will figure this out without her. I do not want her to put herself in danger," I say.

I look up to see Luna Kate standing at the door. "I am good; besides, what kind of friend would I be if I did not help you have this baby," Luna Kate says.

"I really need your help. I have no idea what is happening," I begin to cry.

Luna Kate comes to my bedside. "I have been through this a few times, and I have helped deliver several babies, so I think we will be just fine, okay," Luna Kate says.

"First thing I need is to check and see how far you are, and while I do that, I am going to send Alpha Sebastian to get me a few things for when the baby comes, okay," Luna Kate says.

"Okay," I answer her.

The pain is so great I can barely understand what Luna Kate is saying to Alpha Sebastian as she gives him the list of things she needs to deliver my baby. "Alanis?" Luna Kate calls out to me.

"Yes, sorry, I am in so much pain," I say.

"We have to get you ready. I need to undress you so that I can check on you and the baby," Luna Kate says.

My ears are ringing. "Alanis Alanis Alanis," Luna Kate calls out to me. Something is wrong. I remember what the dark one said; he said that elite wolves die in childbirth.

Luna Kate is talking, but it echoes around me. I can hear Alpha Sebastian and Luna Kate talking now, and the two of them are undressing me. "Stay with me," Alpha Sebastian says.

"I am okay," I say, but it feels like it is just a whisper leaving my lips.

I feel some pressure and a huge pain. "ARGGHHH!" I scream out.

"The baby is coming," Luna Kate says.

"Alanis," Alpha Sebastian says.

I hear someone else in the house, Alpha Erick maybe, but he is not in the room, and he is arguing with someone, and someone is crying. What is happening? I hear little feet running. "Belle," I call out to her. She runs to me. She is trying to get to me and crying to get to me; that is what I am hearing.

"She needs me, and her son needs me," Little Belle says. She places her hand on my stomach and pushes her light into me. She removes the pain, and I begin to feel normal. I can hear again, and I am not entirely out of it.

"Thank you," I say to her.

"It is time to push, Alanis. Belle, go stay with your father; you can come back after the baby is born," Luna Kate says sternly to Little Belle. Little Belle leaves me, but first, she kisses me on the cheek and smiles.

"Alanis, I need you to push with everything you got. This baby is ready to be born," Luna Kate says. Alpha Sebastian holds my hand as I push to bring our child into this world. After about ten minutes, a cry rings out in the room, and our baby is born. It is the most joyous sound I have ever heard in my life.

"We did it," I say to Alpha Sebastian.

"You did it," Alpha Sebastian says. He leans in and kisses my lips.

"It is a boy," Luna Kate exclaims as she examines my son. I am so exhausted, but I reach out to hold him. She cuts his cord, wraps him in a blanket, and then hands him to me. I look down at the most precious thing I have ever seen in my life, my son, my beautiful perfect son.

"He is perfect. What do you want to name him?" Alpha Sebastian says.

"He looks just like you. Aria Sebastian is his name," I say. He does look just like Alpha Sebastian. He is so perfect.

Luna Kate works to clean me up and the room. "I am going to go out and give the two of you some privacy, but when you feel like company, let me know," Luna Kate says.

"Let Belle in for a minute; it is fine," I say. Luna Kate goes to the door and opens it so that Little Belle can come into the room. She rushes over to see the new baby. She looks at him and smiles.

"Hello, little prince," she says. He opens his eyes and looks at her. The two share a moment. I look up at Luna Kate. I can hear voices ringing in my ear. Luna Kate hears them too, and she covers her ears.

The voices stop. "What just happened?" I ask.

"We are the future," Little Belle says.

"How do you know? He is just a baby, and you are just a little girl?" I ask her.

"The weeping wolf told me," Belle answers.

My son and Belle will unite our packs and rule over both territories. That is why the dark one called him the Alpha King. "Long Live the Alpha King and Queen," I whisper.

This story will continue in April 2022 The Alpha's Caged Pet 3
Other book tied to this story
The Alpha's Virgin Slave Book 5 The Weeping Wolf March 2022
The Alpha's Virgin Slave Book 6 April 2022 Legacy (Belle and Aria's story)
Follow me on facebook for updates Lillith Mykals Kennedy, author

Also by Lillith Mykals Kennedy

The Alpha's Caged Pet
The Alpha's Caged Pet Book 2
The Alpha's Caged Pet

The Vampire Authority
I Belong to a Wolf
The Auction

Standalone
Dirty Little Secret
Flames In The Fire
Her Obsession
The Alpha's Fairy
The Auction Series